THE SMITHY MIRACLES

With much
love
Denis

THE SMITHY MIRACLES

J. Denis Glover

iUniverse, Inc.
New York Lincoln Shanghai

The Smithy Miracles

iUniverse, Inc.

For information address:
iUniverse, Inc.
2021 Pine Lake Road, Suite 100
Lincoln, NE 68512
www.iuniverse.com

ISBN: 0-595-30987-9 (pbk)
ISBN: 0-595-75965-3 (cloth)

Printed in the United States of America

To Sydney,
Stone, Field, Blair, Alex

All is subjective.

—Milton Simon

To the Reader

In 1946 I met blacksmith George Lawton by his forge in Churchland, Virginia—worlds away from now in time, culture, and belief systems. Uncle George had served in a long-passed war and was a beloved and spiritual man of timeless dimension.

Within Lawton's memory, calamity had befallen the Great Dismal Swamp some miles south of Churchland—a dramatic and pathetic ruination described vividly to me by his sister-in-law Myra, who does not appear in this book. Hers is another story.

George Melvin Lawton, his son—here called "Sonny"—and the charm and mystery of Tidewater Virginia have haunted me ever since. There I met poverty and prejudice. There I learned what "ancient" meant. And there I met my first person who had encountered a ghost.

Sonny, George, and Myra are buried next to each other in Elmwood Cemetery in Norfolk. Of these real people, events, memories, and beliefs, this book has been widely fabricated.

CHAPTER 1

"You're so black, you're blue," the game warden said, smoothing his sun-bleached hair.

Sonny took Lumpkin's words as a friendly opener. He let two crab lines go, wiped his hands on worn overalls, folded them in his lap, and shifted his eyes from the shallow water to the warden's flat-bottom skiff.

"Black as God," he answered. "Black as that."

"Want to take you out. Ain't safe here, an' you with no food to mention." Lumpkin removed his mirrored sunglasses. "Cain't farm it. Cain't much fish these days. You're no hunter. Got no gun. 'Sides, the land's one perfect tinder box of peat."

Sonny thought of the vast swamp he loved, the forested hammocks, the jungle-like thicknesses, the yellow-green meadows filled with deer. He pictured the springs and sloughs, the open grasses by the creek. The immense aloneness.

"Take me?"

"Take you to the A.M.E. Church downriver. You want, I even git you overland to Moyock or Coinjock or Barco."

Sonny grinned. His face glowed with innocence like the brow of a white-tailed doe. Bushy gray hair framed his crown and crept down the sides of his cheeks, where a beard had never grown. He had known only Cherokees with such a lack of facial hair and wondered at times if some ancestor might have been one.

"My folks Virginians. If'n I went, it'd be Virginia."

"Ain't been out since I knowed you."

Sonny joined his fingertips in front of him. "Left there, let's see…"

"Forgit it! You're Carolina. Been here all *my* life, least. You're a Tarheel."

Sonny still stared at the gunwale of Lumpkin's boat. "Virginian. Mama an' Papa were," he said sadly. He blinked both eyes. "An' the others…" Sonny's hands fell and lay still in his lap.

"What 'others'?"

"If'n I goes out, I goes out north to Virginia. But I gotta home right here." He gestured behind him with his head, not lifting his eyes. "No warden know this place like me. No hunter. This place an' me's friends. Hurricane, dry spells, snow—don't make no matter."

The warden's outboard churned mud, and he killed it, lingering in the channel off the rickety pier.

"Are there folks care about you?"

"Somebody might," Sonny answered.

"You have family?"

Sonny gazed down toward the eelgrass lining the once-brackish creek. "In Churchland."

"Churchland? Where's Churchland?"

Sonny thought back about his childhood town—a land of honeysuckle, trumpet vine, and crepe myrtles, of friends and relatives, of creek christenings, weddings with white cloth over brown skin, burials in red clay—people known for their goodness and skill.

His eyes returned to the gunwale. "Up to Portsmouth," he answered. A sulfurous breeze puffed up the creek, swirling the eelgrass, but leaving the water surface undisturbed. It separated the heat, which made two walls on each side of him, then collapsed together.

Lumpkin straightened his shoulders and put his glasses back on. The boat bobbed as he shifted. "Could probably put you on a bus at South Mills through Chesapeake to Portsmouth. Could you git to Churchland from there?"

"Wouldn't know."

The warden grinned and shook his head.

"How long since you seen this 'somebody'?"

Another breeze came along the creek from the opposite direction. Sonny lowered his hands and touched the two crab lines. His arms ached. He had no concern that the crabs would scatter from the boat or creep down into the mud. They had long since disappeared downstream. He was crabbing from habit.

"Where *you* from, warden?"

"All these years, Sonny, an' I said to call me 'A. R.'"

"Where you from?"

"Sligo."

"See. You're Carolina. I'm Virginia."

"Okay," the warden answered, appearing frustrated. "So what about the bus? I'll pay for the bus myself."

"Never been on one. Wouldn't know about it."

"Oh, sure you have. You been on a bus. How'd you git in here to begin with?"

Sonny began to tow up a line, knotted together from pieces of frayed string and twine he had found floating downcreek on incoming currents. He rolled it around one hand.

"Ran first, then walked," he said, watching the line drip. "Most I remember is hurryin' on alongside the peanuts. Dug 'em an' ate 'em all the way to the swamp. Feastin' it was." He smiled at the thought. "Appreciate you askin'."

This time a blistering movement of air pushed right from the swamp itself, and Lumpkin scouted for it. The heat moved nothing, but surrounded the two men. He tried again.

"Sonny, you're too ole to walk outta here. Swamp's changed. Land's all changed. Nothin' but city 'tween here an' Portsmouth once you git out the Dismal. Peanuts is gone."

Sonny thought about peanuts for a time while the warden waited. The fields had stretched for miles—all the way to Suffolk and beyond. *Just like beans, they were.* He dug them and ate handful after handful and never got thirsty they were so moist. He could not imagine the warden told the truth.

"I'll manage," he said at last.

"You're my last stop, Sonny. Night's afallin'." Pushing with an oar, the warden poled the boat around to face downstream. Sonny continued to roll the first line as he pulled and in a minute laid it on the pier by his leg. The warden hesitated, "What you eatin', Sonny?"

"Think I gotta eat what white folks eats? what people out there eats? Think I don't got my own food?"

Lumpkin changed his tack. "Sonny, how ole are you? When did you come here anyway? You know why you come here?"

Sonny started on the second crab line. Hand-by-hand, foot-by-foot he pulled it out and began winding it around the knuckles of one hand.

"Papa was a water boy at Cold Harbor." His head jerked up with the flash of memory.

"What you mean?" the warden said, astonished.

"For the Grand Army."

"Your daddy was at Cold Harbor?"

"Yes-*suh*! For the Grand Army."

"Which was that?"

"The Grand Army of Northern Virginia." He paused. "Or the Grand Army of the Potomac. Don't know."

"You're tellin' me your daddy served in the *Civil War*?"

Sonny curled the last foot of line around his hand, took it off, and laid it on top of the other. He placed his arms behind him on the pier and leaned back to watch the darkening sky, washed above in peach. He knew the creek well—how it flowed southerly into Corapeake Ditch, which ran into Dismal Swamp Canal, which led to the Pasquotank River, and eventually to Albemarle Sound.

"I'm tellin' you all that an' more, but nobody was drinkin' no water that day," he answered.

"You're tellin' me your daddy was in the Army?"

"Cold Harbor. Cold as hell for them that's adyin'."

"Do you have any idea what that means?"

"I 'spec' you never know such sufferin'." Another pillow of heat pushed out of the dry swamp. Sonny wiped his face and looked in that direction.

"Knowed they's dead before they's shot," he continued. "Papa brought drinkin' water. An' they knowed they was goin' over 'cuz they pin names on themself so's they'd be sent home to the folks. Knowed they was dead before the boys shot one shot."

Another breeze blew upstream from the southeast in gusty breaths. Gulls sailed on a high current. Mosquitoes and gnats swarmed in the twilight air, chased by swallows and purple martins.

"Think on it, Sonny. I could git back to you."

"No need, warden. I'm here, an' I'm here 'til I cain't do nothin' about it."

"Well…we'll see," answered Lumpkin. "I jis' have a feelin'…I care, Sonny." He started the outboard and glanced over his shoulder as he turned the boat away from the setting sun. "See you!" he said with a casual wave as he revved the motor. Sonny nodded, but said nothing.

The sun had fallen in tangerine flames behind cloud strings as the warden's boat disappeared. Sonny watched mists envelop the boat until the only spot visible was the warden's straw hat and straw hair reflecting sunlight over his dark collar.

He gathered the two rolls of string and worked to get his feet under him. He tucked one knee in and pushed up with the opposite foot, the joints cracking. He stopped to enjoy the sunset and the closing mists, highlighted here and there by a sunbeam.

Then, fingering the string, he walked slowly along toward a makeshift shelter that sat on a hammock above the creek, umbrellaed by an ancient live oak.

CHAPTER 2

How'd you git in here to begin with? The warden's words echoed as Sonny stepped along the path.

He remembered another oak tree, Camp Meeting Oak. He had played under its large arms when in dank childhood nights his mother had hauled him there. She never missed Camp Meeting with Preacher Merriot, whose strong hands and arms had earned him the title, "Hammer of God." He would call for Jesus' living presence—cleansing neighbors' sins by scaring them bug-eyed, promising salvation through the blood of the Lamb.

"'Are you ready,' say the Master, 'to be crucify with me?'" Merriot sang out, raising his giant fist and whipping it in front of him.

"Yes, Lord, we ready!" Sonny's neighbors returned.

"Does you feel the ground acreepin' around you, jis' like the Master?"

"We feels it, Preach' Merriot. We feels the ground acreepin' around. We *feels* it!"

"Is *Jee*-sus your pilot, apoling you through the swamp of sin?"

"Yes, Preacher, Lord Jesus be the pilot! Yes, Preacher. Yes, *Jee*-sus! Yes, *Jee*-sus! Yes, *Jee*-sus!"

Then out from the Tidewater underbrush would float twelve townswomen wearing white chicken-feather wings and chanting, "Glory, glory, Hallelujah!

Glory to the saved in the Lord! Crucifi', ris'n, comin' agin! Comin' agin! Comin' agin! Glory, *glory*, Hallelujah!"

Sonny landed under a bench and shook like a dog in a thunderstorm. Even when he returned home in the nights and the angels gossiped among themselves and he knew they were mothers of friends, he still trembled and hid behind his mother's skirt. Preacher Merriot never seemed to Sonny to arrive or leave, but just stood there under that tree.

But the last night, when everybody left but Sonny and Mama, Merriot became something else.

"Stay a spell," he coaxed as he pressed close to Sonny's mother. "Come on, set a spell. Right here." He pulled at Mama's elbow, put his arm around her waist.

"Goin' home, Preacher," Mama answered.

"No, you wants to be with me." His hand crept tighter around her waist.

"Don't need me!" she said.

"Yes, I do. An' you needs me. You know you do. I can help you out," he said as he touched Mama's breasts.

"Stay 'way, Preacher!"

"Now, now," he said and pulled her into him.

"Git off me, Preacher!" Mama yelled and turned her head toward Sonny. "Run, boy, run!"

Sonny ripped at the Preacher like a dog tearing a rag toy. A painful slap to the boy's head sent him into the brush.

As he returned to the hut now, his thoughts resisted what followed. He saw Preacher's leering eyes, heard Mama's cries of pain as Preacher twisted her arms and began to take her. And her contorted face as she tried to hide herself.

"Run, Sonny, run! Don't you never come back! Run to the swamp an' stay! Stay in the swamp! Don't never come back here!"

Raising his fist, the Preacher struck down on Mama's face at the back of her jaw. The thud of the blow came with a crack of bone, and her head seemed to Sonny to separate from her body. Her eyelids fluttered as she slumped to the ground, and her eyes rolled back when she landed. He had seen people die, and he knew Mama had been killed.

Sonny tore through the brambles, down the Norfolk and Western rails, and into the wide-ranging farmland to the south. He foraged as he went and finally arrived at the swamp miles away. Here he remained, never to return, even to his father.

Through the years Sonny grew to love the Great Dismal, a sweeping, desolate land for strangers, but refuge and home to him. He taught himself how to survive in the close safety of its woods and grasslands, and along its creeks.

He rambled through its vastness in Virginia and North Carolina where the forest at times grew right from the water. Trees sometimes shot up in colossal columns, a hundred- to two-hundred feet. But in places slash cutting of the white cedars, called "junipers" by the locals, had carved out broad patches of wasteland. Still, cypress, swamp maple, black gum—the Creeks from farther south called it "tupelo"—and tulip poplar waved abundantly above the swamp with holly and dogwood under.

At ground level clusters of gall-bushes flourished, mingled with honey-suckle, grapevines, brier, and laurel, often forming impenetrable thicket. High creepers hung from the top branches of trees to the ground so that Sonny would have to part them like curtains. And here and there thorns of prickly ash, the devil's walking stick, would tear his skin.

A farmer told him once that before the Civil War the swamp had given refuge to escaping slaves, and that the state had allowed their murder. A jury would guess the dead slave's value, the sheriff paying two-thirds to the owner. One day Sonny had even found a crumpled "Proclamation of Outlawry" in an abandoned church and given it to Lumpkin to read. The warden confirmed that the swamp had thronged with Negro-hunting parties skilled at sharp shooting—with howling dogs experienced at the hunt. Sonny knew there would have been a time when he might have been the quarry.

During the spring Sonny wandered through walls of pink and white laurel. Yellow jessamine swung in the air, perfuming the undergrowth. Flowering vines with names only an expert would know mosaicked the interior. He waded through cow lilies, jewelweed, ranges of field flowers, and uncountable varieties of seed-bearing reeds and grasses that swept the forest edges like bristles on a paintbrush.

Sometimes he came upon Lake Drummond, which bubbled up on the Virginia side, and numberless fresh-water ponds, and sloughs dotted or criss-crossed the swamp surface. For years he had wandered among the cypress and red cedar that had attracted lumbermen and shingle-getters in the past, bringing rail tracks, mills, and shacks with them.

Sonny came upon their remnants on almost every trek away from his creek-side shanty. Beside the shinglers' huts, open-sided sheds canopied rusted remains of shingle machines, crouching like raptors in molding caves. On the east and south sides, small-scale railroads had transported the shingles to market. On the north they had been floated by lighter up the Nansemond River not far from Churchland toward the Chuckatuck and out into the wide James. In years gone by, hammocks and drained farm fields had provided the only dry land, but so much of the swamp had been channelized that large regions dried to peat, once used for fuel, now good for little but subsistence gardening.

On his treks Sonny would spot beavers working to dam water, making homes for themselves and basking turtles and muskrats. Catfish and crappie populated every stream, supplying him with meat. And each stretch of water was home to herons and kingfishers he had come to love while blue jays and ravens screamed through the forest. Pine siskins and orioles would hop through low cover to perch on his hut.

A region of heat and moisture and fertility, Sonny saw how the swamp had taken back what men had wrested from it. Outsiders had to cut and recut winding paths. Ditches that sliced across the trails and threw the scent away from hounds had to be recleared and dredged, but Sonny knew the natural passways and seldom disturbed a twig. Lumbermen said the sweet air and spring water served like tonics and would keep Sonny from swamp disease. And the climate so suited him that the air and water became his only medicine.

In his wandering he found where pioneers had cleared fields for corn, tobacco, and cotton on the swamp edges, but most lay abandoned. He had crossed homesteads where they had felled huge trees and dragged them to the borders, the framework of branches interlaced with Virginia creeper billowing over the branches like green waves, and the decayed trunks formed islands of compost in the old fields. Long-absent farmers had fenced the clearings against deer only to be conquered by kudzu and pine, and Sonny was glad to have the farmers gone.

Soon after arriving in the Great Dismal, Sonny built his shelter by the creek below the Virginia line. To hold it together he wove lianas around boards from oyster-shucker shacks and box parts that drifted along the ditches. He anchored the shelter to the ground with lianas over the top tied to trunk stubble.

He rainproofed the roof by wedging rusted tin sheets under the lianas, sheets he had stripped off a shingler's Quonset hut and carried for miles along the creek. Flexible with little resistance to the wind, the shelter had withstood years of hurricanes, even though fierce rains pierced the porous walls.

The shelter door opened toward the creek on the north. The front and back walls each had a crude window for what breezes arose. At one end Sonny built a simple fireplace of stones gathered on his wide-ranging walks through the borderlands.

Opposite the fireplace he put together a wooden pallet, covered with pads of dried grass, one to sleep on and one to cover him. Two broken chairs and a board table from a logger's ruin provided the only other furnishings. The table held his pots, pans, and utensils, including knives and skewers for dressing and roasting rabbit, opossum, and fish.

Sonny snared rabbits with a loop trap and hooked fish with a line tied to a worm-baited safety pin. The opossum he just ran after when spotted in the late evenings. For half the year he also ate berries, persimmons, peaches, nuts, and apples, and he kept a crock of spring water from a neighboring hammock. He would scrape up the parts of a rabbit or fish he could not use and carry them back of the hut to share with rodents, crows, and bobcats.

One day a small redtail hawk flew down to the offal, and the two eyed each other for the better part of a half-hour. Three days later when Sonny left the shelter, hands full of fur and guts, the hawk sat on the tip of a dead pine. After that, on more occasions than not, the redtail showed itself, ate, and left nothing any creature but an ant would want.

The game warden gone, Sonny entered the hut, hanging the crab strings on the wall. He took a long drink from the crock, picked up a worm-eaten apple, and sat down on his pallet to eat. Heat current after heat current pressed through the shanty walls without moving a leaf on the live oak tree and lay on Sonny like a suffocating comforter.

He got up, went to the door, and, peering into the growing darkness, tossed the apple core out. He paused. Something across the wild expanse made him uneasy. A knife of salt air pierced the night; the heat fell in again. He looked up and down the twilight creek, trying to read the night.

"All right out here, I guess," he said and returned to his bunk. "All right."

Taking off overalls and threadbare shirt, he sat on the pallet edge again, staring through the door and feeling the heat press his naked body, his hands gripping the pallet frame. He studied the night and the air shifts. A streak of heat lightning flashed pink in the northeast, silhouetting a cloud ridge.

His eyelids weighed heavy, and he slid the crisp grass mattress onto the floor to sleep on the wood frame for coolness. But when he lay down, even that pressed hot against his back. He listened deep into the bat-filled forest. The crickets and the great horned owl hushed.

The swamp had never been so quiet.

CHAPTER 3

Before daybreak Sonny roused from his pallet and knew something had changed. The June bugs were silent. No gulls circled the brush by the hut. No blackbirds cawed. He pulled on his shirt and overalls, picked up a frayed pair of sneakers he had found in the piney woods, and, barefoot, shuffled to the shelter door.

The wind had begun to blow out of the southeast. It erupted in fitful gusts, yet never directly from the south. Sonny had always been able to read the wind. Today was different.

He brushed wisps of hair back along the sides of his head with one hand and, craning his neck around, peered at the horizon. Looking. Sensing. Nothing seemed quite the same. For a while, he stood by the hut, motionless, waiting for a sign. Finding none, he paced along the path toward the creek.

And then it came. The earth warmed his feet, and, as they sank into the spongy peat, they almost burned. Never had the earth been so hot so early in the morning. He moved farther down to cool his soles in the creek. Sliding them into the ooze—the creek was too warm.

Puzzled, Sonny stepped onto the pier, which shuddered under him, and pondered. He slid his feet back onto the peat, then back into the water, and again back onto the pier, testing. He repeated the trial, sweating in the premature heat, as the sky whitened on the eastern horizon, giving shape to the pitch pines and grasses.

He sat down on the pier to slip on the sneakers. As he rested there, still wondering in the early light, he heard a thrashing from beyond the shelter. Unseen, it stopped momentarily when he looked, then continued in his direction when he looked away. But when he looked again, a blackened puma leapt into the clearing near him. Fixing on Sonny, the crazed cat screamed, twisting its head with terrified eyes, and raced down the path toward the pier.

"Oh, my God!" Sonny whispered. Rock-still, he prepared himself for pain. The puma came on strong—but short of the pier jumped wide and flung itself into the low water, twisting and rolling and lapping. It finally came to rest on its stomach, panting and staring north across the creek.

Near the hut a frantic deer herd jumped into the air and fled like grasshoppers toward the water's edge. The puma paid no attention to either Sonny or the deer, which splashed into the creek and at last stood erect, lifting noses to the wind. Sonny had seen them singly or with a fawn or two, but never together in this strange migration.

Then he remembered the danger next to him.

"Oh, my God!" he whispered again and took a few cautious steps, first off the boards of the pier, next back toward the shelter, never taking his eyes from the puma, which still showed no interest.

"I never seen—" Sonny said, guardedly backing up the path.

No sooner had he turned toward his shanty than he froze. Against the shelter's splintery boards a black bear loomed eight feet high on hind legs, shaking the hut's feeble walls. Baring its bright canines, the giant lumbered toward him. Reaching the end of the path, it pushed Sonny over with one powerful sway, made its way to the water, and fell in, sending rhythmic waves over the panting puma.

Sonny saw his chance and ran gimp-leggedly into the hut, closing the sagging door behind.

"Father in heaven, what'll I do?" he murmured. He peeked between the door slats at the inexplicable sight of all these natural enemies in the creek, ignoring one another as the morning light broke and other terrified creatures joined them. The wind still blew in the erratic way that had no meaning for him, and the earth continued to heat under his feet.

As the sun rose, the animals became more restive. Soon Sonny heard commotion through the dry vegetation behind the shelter, a widespread stir like a broom brushing in a constant thrashing of bristles. Upstream and downstream, more deer leapt into the creek. A brown bear with her cub hobby-horsed through the low reeds. Bobcats screeched just out of sight.

Vegetation everywhere bounced alive with a widespread parade of swamp creatures—chipmunks, raccoons, opossums, lizards, snakes, turtles—all heading north toward the creek, gathering there, crowding, wading in. The grass vibrated with fleeing life, oblivious of the danger each might pose to the other.

A whir sounded above, the beating of hundreds of wings, as the swamp birds flew out into the brightening northern clouds. Herons, pelicans, hawks, and vast floats of smaller birds filled the sky until it turned gray as twilight.

His sneaker soles smelled of rubber on the baking peat as Sonny peered out. His ears rang with the swelling clamor, his nostrils and mouth dry. He could not account for anything; it had never happened before. And he waited for some built-in wisdom to tell him what to do.

As noon approached with no letup of the exodus, Sonny heard explosions, louder than any collection of tree falls or shotgun firings—regular, echoing, thundering. The heat built in his sneakers, but he tied the shoestrings in anticipation of flight, wiping his face across the tattered sleeve of his T-shirt.

The wind shifted and roared directly out of the south—steadily, with purpose. The smell of burning, followed by the thick smoke of flaming peat, invaded the hut and roiled up into the sky, turning it black. The explosions came nearer. The earth steamed.

Sonny found it hard to breathe. Tears and soot smeared his face, and sweat saturated his clothes. He turned to the rear of the shelter, and, squinting between two boards, searched south through the hammock beyond scattered pines to the cedar forest.

His eyes grew large as he saw a wall of steam rising in the distance and a higher wall of smoke curling up behind it, whipping in his direction. A pitch pine popped into flame, then another some feet away from it, then a whole grove—contrasting orange against the white and black walls behind.

"Got to go, uh-huh! Got to find Papa back to Churchland!"

Except for Lumpkin's urging, the idea had not occurred to him over the years. Nor the thought that Papa might be long dead. But something inside him pulled, something more than flight from the fire itself.

"Now!"

He returned to the door and stepped out, afraid and unafraid at the same time.

The puma moved first. Slowly rising, it took two steps farther into the creek, then bounded across, half swimming, and disappeared into the thicket toward the north. The bear got up and swayed after. As if on their command, the others followed, some wading, some swimming. Like a flesh rug, the animal troop migrated, hell-bent for safety, overflown by flocks of birds and the streaming steam and smoke.

In the short interval it took for Sonny to reach the creek, wildlife had overspread it. He joined them as a fleeing partner. Leaning over and pointing his hands together, spreading them out again, he made place for himself on the creek surface and walked in, slipping up to his shoulders here and there into a muddy hole, but moving steadily forward. Toward the middle he swam in broad cumbersome strokes, lying flat over the narrow channel, his face in hind legs before him.

"I'm with y'all!" Sonny shouted, the water washing over his face. "Time to find Papa agin for sure!"

Thick smoke attacked from above and filled his lungs. He could no longer see where he swam. Ashes and burning leaves skidded over the surface and sizzled into the water, and he dunked as they fell into his hair. A claw grazed his ribs. A furry weight pushed him aside and under, and he choked on the brown water.

Desperately he lurched his right foot forward and found purchase in a clod of bank mud, raising his head up for air. Slipping again, he struggled under the surface, as he pinwheeled his feet up onto the far side.

Breathing heavily, Sonny stepped through the muck and hurried along. Beyond the smoke he saw the ash- and fire-rain igniting patches of dead saw grass and rushes. Fleeing with him—the bears ignoring the rabbits, and the pumas ignoring the chipmunks—the swamp animals dodged to and fro among the bright patches

"Git on! Git on!" Sonny yelled. "Git on!"

He felt at one with them, not fear of any, but pride and hope in the team effort to survive. He did not pause as a bear family overtook him and passed by in the swirling semi-darkness. Raccoons and opossums and chipmunks and foxes bounced forward. The overflights of swamp birds thinned and raced ahead, and solitary birds of prey screeched above.

In front, across the dry bog stretched a wide pitch pine hammock, enveloped in smoke but not yet on fire. Sonny knew it meandered north for miles through the parched swamp. He would find his way to the channelized flat farmland of Tidewater and farther on to Churchland. He yearned for the peanut and soybean fields, for some spring or farmer's sweet well to drink from, and for his ancient father.

A momentary peace came over the creatures as they mounted the low hammock and rested, looking back, scanning forward into the thickness of the wooded brush, then disappearing into it. Sonny took a step onto the incline, stopped for breath and energy, squinting as he searched for an open way through the underbrush he hoped would take him onward. He felt a sense of independence from the animals now, and a conviction that they would make it.

"Goes into the ark two by two, but you goes into heaven one by one," he announced loudly.

A skittish cool breeze pushed aside the smoke, and he glimpsed light through trees toward his right. He picked up a cedar bough, broke it in half, and held it at arm's length for a moment.

"Fine walkin' stick. Fine!"

Setting off, he took slow step after slow step with his new stick, resuming his flight from the fire into the north-wending hammock, and his spirit waxed into confidence.

"The King's highway, an' the traffic light am green!"

CHAPTER 4

Sonny did not know where or when the firestorm had first ignited, or who had started it. He had seen loggers and shinglers heaping unusable limbs and tending their bonfires for days, and farmers scorching fields in the fall, trusting some ditch to boundary the fire. And hunters, fishers, and sightseers built campfires and tossed cigarettes into the underbrush. Lumpkin had said that careless young campers thought they played in their own private wetland impervious to flame.

Sonny had, indeed, watched the bogs quench their fires, and sometimes the blaze would run over or through the ground and disappear for want of sear touchwood or peat. He had seen ash sail through the air and fall dead at the edge of some pool or lake. Once flames had risen in walls to the border of a shingle company's clearcut and burned there for an hour or two, dwindling to smoke and spent ash.

But he knew the Great Dismal was deep peat, and a fire in the heart could smolder for months and inch along underground to flash up miles away in a parched copse of brown needles. He knew that a match lit by the banks of the Pasquotank might kindle a field fire far to the northwest below Suffolk.

As Sonny persisted along the hammock toward the passway, he saw a rising inferno drifting from the swamp's Carolina side in his direction, and he became terrified. Massive floats of flaming debris erupted from it and streaked through the atmosphere in his direction.

Upper-air currents spun the fire at him—thunderhead towers of smoke, blackening the sky. They edged northeasterly toward Portsmouth and Norfolk, where he knew there were huge military installations. Through the years he had seen the Navy jets flash to and fro above the clouds.

Ash showered down like the first flakes of a blizzard. "Snow in the Southland!" Sonny tried to joke as he entered the slender trail. But he knew from the day's sounds and smells and from the animals' eyes that he had to press on to Lake Drummond. The wildlife had all but disappeared—some apparently feeling secure in the underbrush, some in secret wet coves of safety. And some advanced far beyond him.

As the ash fell heavily, Sonny hurried through groves of second-growth timber into less and less familiar lands. Burning leaves floated down into every clearing, carving circles of orange and black on the turf. His eyes wept again, and he breathed the dense air with increasing effort.

Coming upon a pool bounded by laurel, he drank lustily, then scraped up moss matting from a log to tie over his mouth and nostrils with a piece of new-growth willow. As a child, he had created such a mossman mask to frighten his friends, breathing freely through the moist green filtration. Now it would save his lungs.

Pushing on, Sonny crossed the narrow-gauge Richmond Cedar Works railbed that ran east to the Dismal Swamp Canal. He knew shinglers from there used to load shakes on the cars for market. When he first arrived in the swamp, they had used a full-gauge train or a canal barge, but later flatbed trucks took the shingles to the branches of the Elizabeth. He sensed he was now in Virginia and felt safe even as a loblolly exploded down the tracks.

"I'm acomin', Papa!" Sonny announced and busily made his way over the railroad clearing to a path angling north. It stabbed into a mixed forest of slash pines, oak, swamp maples, and black walnuts, understoried with yellowing sumac and bramble. He burrowed into its thickness and traveled over acre upon acre, where the falling sparks died out high in the treetops.

As he fell into an immense fern bog dammed by beavers, the sparks lit only an occasional leaf, which withered into the water or moist peat. The trail ran from mound to mound and stump to stump around the beaver pond, and Sonny bounced heavily through the broad lowland, uncertain of the trail, and stopped for a moment to remoisten the mask.

As the path lifted out of the beaver dam, it bore through a hemlock grove out into sapling-spotted fields. The air pressed hotly down, and grass patches flickered and smoldered evilly. Sonny grew tired, even though walking proved less strenuous. He began to pace himself, following the clear path, which became a deer track in a straight line across the openness. As he traveled mile after mile, he occasionally frightened a rabbit or woodchuck caught off guard. The path wandered from one natural pasture to another, and the fire followed.

Suddenly, without any special drop of flame, a rampart of fire rose from Sonny's right, circled behind him, lashed around to his left. Before he could spit, the entire grassland reared up with heat so searing it could not have been caused by burning grass alone, but erupted from the peat base itself.

Sonny remembered a similar thing when he had been a boy. One windy night, Uncle Arabo had fallen asleep with a lit cigar on a tapestry divan in the four-room cabin. Nothing had happened for hours until Aunt Leotta smelled smoke and woke Arabo up. Only a thin wisp wiggled its way between the cushions and into the air. There appeared no immediate threat, but Aunt Leotta ran for a broom to beat it out.

Raising the broom, she broke a window, and the wind came driving in. The heated air, fed by the wind, ignited one wall instantly, the fire washing gently from that wall to the next. In less than five minutes, the fire engulfed the cabin became engulfed, leaving Uncle Arabo and Aunt Leotta homeless.

Now Sonny's landscape quietly sprang into flame with the fanning wind until the crackling turned to a hollow roar like whistling without pursing the lips. The soft roar turned loud when the fiery land reached up to the fire-clouds as Sonny had seen lightning reach up from the earth to touch the lightning from the sky.

"Save me, Lord, ere I perish!" Sonny screamed as he barreled blindly through the fire toward the woods beyond. Burning thatch flew in the wind and sailed into his hair. He swept it off and pulled the moss mask up over his head to moisten his scalp. His bog-wet shirt and overalls steamed his body, and he thought the near-boiling moisture of his own clothing might scald him.

Ahead, the woods reared up in tulip trees with rotted vegetation below, and a west wind whipped up from nowhere as if the giant trees had created their own weather. Spared for the moment, Sonny strayed wildly among the thick columns, flailing his cedar stick, searching for a way. He wound around, focusing on what might be north. Sparks penetrated the tulips, but the ground passed easy underfoot, no rocks, little brush. He plunged on until at last he came upon a cartway.

"Thank you, brother Jesus!" he exclaimed to the tall wilderness and walked into it with hands overhead with praise.

"Yes! Through the Red Sea an' out the fiery furnace, I say."

Soon the wind came from the west again, clearing the purple sky. Sonny sensed a reprieve. The tulipwoods turned to tall pine with an understory of berried dogwood. Evening fell agreeable here—the dark of nature, not of smoke.

The cartway stretched on until it deteriorated into a path by a pool and three hickory trees. Sonny wandered over to the pool and threw away his mask. He knelt down to cup water to his mouth and splash it on his face and hair. He had not eaten all day and scrabbled among the hickory mast for any nuts that had not been home to worm or rot. He soon had handfuls.

"Dinner's where you finds it," he said, chuckling.

He stretched out on the ground, propping himself on one elbow, and broke the shells with small rocks. He laid his head on his outstretched arm, wondering how his life could ever return, wondering if he would ever find Papa and what Papa would say if he did.

As evening drew down, Sonny got up and ambled along the narrower path through dense pitchpines. Though moist, the heavy needle cover would make a better bed than leaves, he thought. Walking on, he saw a weathered tent platform and gathered needles from under the pines and heaped them onto it, then lowered himself to the edge and rocked over onto them.

As he settled, Sonny was surprised to see the stars through the boughs. For years, they had been his companions and comfort, and here they were, still silent above.

He thought about the game warden. Was he safe? Had the fire started near Elizabeth City and blown north? And his shelter? And the dock? And all the creatures he knew and loved?

A small shadow briefly covered his view. A sprig bent, and he heard the tender night-scree of a hawk and knew it was his redtail.

CHAPTER 5

In the morning heavy smoke mounted in the air. Sonny pushed on through piney woods to groves of pin oaks, leaves curling against the fall. Clearings ranged high with seed-bearing grass, weed, and thistle. Where the southern wind had blown sparks, small fires burned, but soon the welcome smell of lake water caught his nostrils. The land became marshy, and massive cypress trees spread their trunks into the ooze.

He stared through them onto Lake Drummond, the tannin-colored Great Dismal center, fed by Cypress Swamp to the west. The sparse cypress lifted their feathery boughs like relaxed fingers. Their knees and cut trunks dotted the lake for a hundred feet out. Stepping onto a section of sandy shore, Sonny knelt, scooped up the water, and drank.

He continued along a feeder ditch and skirted the east side of the lake, where he glimpsed the redtail hawk, fluttering back and forth on the horizon. The earlier drive to push on returned with a force—no longer just the need to escape the fire, but the need to see his father, a need he had never felt before. It had been planted by Lumpkin's questions, but there also came an overwelling from some mystery within. What had become of his mother's body? How had his father grieved for her? for him? Was Papa even still there? He wanted desperately to find out.

Beyond the redtail, Sonny saw a buzzard band swirling in the sky, three to the right, two to the left. "Somethin's adyin'," he said to himself. "Some somethin's adyin'." He approached whatever it was through a sapling forest and over a thistle ridge.

"Lord!" he whispered as he crept down toward a watering hole in a trampled pasture. Black wings boiled in tight groups. He broke into a hop and twirled the walking stick above his head.

"You-whee!"

Still running, he let the stick fly into the mass.

"You-whee!"

The birds lifted laboriously as he hopped down the hill and careened into the watering hole, kicking water and mud toward a buzzard on the opposite shore.

"Git! Git! Git!" he yelled, threatening with his arms. The bird ran a few steps, took to the air, and joined the others in a slow circle.

The stench of carnage choked Sonny more than the smoke he had been fleeing. Parts of a snowy egret, its feathers blasted in all directions, lay half-in, half-out, of the reddened water. Sonny waded over and fished for the body, but caught only a long hooked neck attached to a bloody clump of feathers and vertebrae.

Sonny turned to the remains of a blue heron pair, one set of yellow eyes fixed on him. Four brown pelicans lay piled together as if comforting each other in death. An osprey was splayed beyond, and a saw whet owl's head sat on the shore like a bowling ball. All but unrecognizable smaller birds, displays of fanned and broken feathers, scattered the perimeter, where boot and hoof prints had pressed into the drying mud.

Why somebody kill these po' creatures, jis' seekin' refuge from fire? Sonny wondered

Around the pool edges and joining at the far side, he saw slide trails of heavily matted grasses, stained with blood. Catching his breath as he left the water, he followed the trail. Shoulders slumped, he walked until the grasses grew tall, cut by a four-foot wide channel of broken reeds. Following patches of blood, he continued a hundred yards and came to an abrupt halt.

A collection of dead wildlife lay out as if on a counter: an eight-inch skinning knife stuck through the ribs of a half-skinned puma, two bobcat carcasses, angry eyes open, nestled by five deer, one heavily racked, and a doubled-up black bear. As the sun reached toward noon, Sonny figured the hunters must have broken for lunch. He stepped over to a bobcat, pressed its eyes closed, and patted the fur globe of its head. He did the same for the other animals, putting them to rest.

Tied to a sassafras tree beyond the carcasses, a mule-like hinny shifted nervously. A rope truss trailed behind it, and Sonny realized the hinny must have drawn the animals to this point. He wiped his eyes, stroked the hinny's neck, and climbed over a rail fence to a dirt track. Turning to look once more, he muttered, "God, bless you!" waved gently, and walked down the track.

In the early afternoon he reached a cornfield, stalks dry and broken after harvest. Beyond the field stood a brick ante-bellum mansion, and his throat ached for drink from its well.

"Laws, Laws, Laws," he said as he made his way toward the house. The stalks and leaves crackled; the earth rows crunched under his feet. Grasshoppers flew up in his face, but he shielded his eyes and focused on the once-ornate mansion. Peeling columns decorated the front. Two oversized chimneystacks bookended the sidewalls.

Something his father told him when he was a tike flared up in his mind: a brigade of Tidewater soldiers retreated, like him, from the woods and across the field toward the mansion's grandeur. Canteens bounced at their hips, rifles on their shoulders. He imagined sunlight catching the red and white flag—the countryside colored gray with men, white with cotton, and green with pecan trees.

Sonny moved out of the field and onto a red-clay drive. Shuffling along under the skeletons of branching live oaks, he arrived at the front yard, guarded by walls of purple stream stones. A mailbox with "Tutwiler" on it leaned against one of them. To the right the wall ended in a primitive graveyard plotted out of the corner of the lawn with one broken and one sunken marker.

Looking for a pump, Sonny drew closer. Behind the columns a porch wrapped around the house, where a sofa swing hung on rusted chains. He mounted the central stairs and thought for a moment to rest on the swing. But thirst got the better of him, and he walked to the left, pushed aside the swing, and, feeling with his hand along the side of the building, arrived at an open window.

Peering in, Sonny saw a dusty parlor. A leather-cushioned chair sat by a wooden radio with a yellow, fan-shaped dial. A Chinese checkers set rested on top. Above that, a mirrored box held a blue-robed Jesus, carrying a crook on one arm and a lamb on the other. Jesus' gaze rested on shotguns stacked in the corner. Tiny red and blue straw flowers hid his feet. Sonny had seen such a picture before and recalled the first stanza of an old hymn that appeared on the mirror-frame.

He remembered off-key singing in a bare, country church and a water-streaked print of a woman clinging to a stone cross like a tombstone in the eye of an ocean tempest. "Rock of Ages" it had read.

> My faith looks up to Thee-e-e,
> Thou Lamb of Calvare-e-e,
> Saviour De-e-e-vine;
> Now hear me while I pray-ay-ay,
> Take all my guilt away-ay-ay,
> O let me from this day-ay-ay
> Be wholly-y-y Thine!

Sonny looked beyond the parlor to a half-closed door and into a dim hall-way at the center of the house. A huckleberry globe cast an eerie light about the hall. His stomach tightened as he looked over his shoulder.

Figures stepped around in his mind—he could not remember who they were, but could not release them: A funeral, coffin roped over an open grave. A butchering—scalding pots in crisp fall air—too cold for any smell but that of choking smoke and boiling fat.

He walked around the chimney, heard rumbling, and peered through a floor-length window. A carved table-and-chair set sat solidly in the middle of the room. Sunlight glimmered on cut-glass bowls and silver pitchers atop a sideboard with a wide, beveled mirror.

Then he moved around the corner toward the outbuildings, where weeds and brambles grew untamed at the yard's far perimeter. A cast-iron pump with a chained tin cup rose in the middle, arching over a wooden trough. He stumbled toward it, lifted the handle, and pushed down. The fitting screeched, but four pumpings pulled the water up. He continued to pump with one arm and grabbed the cup with the other.

Suddenly, a shotgun report caught him in midpump, and buckshot tore into the ground. Sonny ducked, and a kennelful of sleepy dogs began yapping, baying, and clawing at their chain-like gate.

The shotgun fired again. The dogs went wild.

"Outta here, nigra!" yelled a heavy-set bearded man as he reloaded.

"Nothin' for you here. Git to hell out!"

A second climbed onto an upper porch and also waved a shotgun. Clean-shaven, but just as fat, he fell to a knee and took aim, resting the gun on the railing.

"You-whoo! Git for sure—or you'll lose what you got left of those legs of yours!"

Sonny twisted and called back.

"Jis' want a drink…"

"Git on, I say!"

Sonny's hand motioned toward the pump.

"Nothin'! Git!" yelled the first man, lowering his gun in Sonny's direction. "What say, Harve, got us a chase, or what?"

"Believe so. Been waitin' for it." He called down to Sonny, "Nowheres to go, nigra. But you can stand there an' die, or you can have a little run. What say?"

"But—" said Sonny.

"But nothin'! Got no 'buts'!"

A gun fired again, and Sonny felt a pellet hit his left side, and he crumpled with the impact, feeling for a wound.

"That's to start," called the window. "Now we're acomin' real slow so's you gotta chance to turn tail." The man laughed a shrill laugh. "Enjoyin' this right much!"

"Why?—" Another cluster of shot puffed pocks in the dust. Sonny flew from disbelief to dread and back to disbelief. A dark memory loomed.

He stood, looking each Tutwiler in the face, wiped his right hand along his bib, and leaned in the direction of safety. The hunters grasped their shotguns and held their heads close to the stocks.

"Off you go, nigra! See you real soon!" called the porch, laughing, then squealing.

CHAPTER 6

Pellets tore past Sonny's head and rattled through the woods beyond. He fell over the pump, sending the cup clanging. An easy target from the house, he ran across the dust and into the woods.

"We'll git you, nigra! Whee-oh! Got us a *chase!*"

A volley tore the underbrush to Sonny's right. He barreled as straight as he could through thin, then thicker, woods. On the rises, blackberry canes tore into his legs. In the dells, damp peat sank beneath his feet, slowing his flight.

Birds erupted from the thickets, and insects swarmed as Sonny splashed out of a bog. Gnats flew into his eyes while snakes and rodents made way. A circling buzzard gang spread black wing feathers.

Another volley sounded, and Sonny stumbled sideways into a flat of gray sand, which sucked at his body. It was not his first fall into quicksand. He resisted the reflex to kick, and splayed over onto his back, spreading his weight and grabbing for brush.

The men's voices moved some distance behind him and to the left, and Sonny knew they were searching off track. "Thank the Lord, they ain' brought the dogs!" he whispered.

He laid his head back and shuffled his body side to side as he grabbed for harder wood lower on the bushes. Leaves ripped off. Smaller stems gave way.

He was losing to the sand. Abandoning the struggle, Sonny looked up through the opening in the leaf cover, caught sight of the redtail, and waited. It had happened to him before, this waiting for the right way to move, but this time he felt the presence of a helper.

Sonny slid a knee toward his chin and turned on his stomach, shifting hands to pull steadily at clusters of stems. They held, and he rolled again, pulling the other knee up under him, and then pulled and rolled until his body edged onto hard ground. He lay there covered in fine sticky sand, conscious that his hunters might find him at any moment.

Before long he heard the men's distant voices laughing like geese, then a high-pitched hoot. They were fanning out to the left of him, so Sonny rose to his feet, circled the pit, and moved off to the right where he took up the run through underbrush and thick woods.

He heard the hawk scree as he entered a hemlock grove, the ground moist and cushioned. Ahead, trailing down a shady gully, lay seven stone cisterns eight feet across, half above ground level, each connected to the other by rubber tubing, wide mossy boards on top protecting the water from falling leaves and needles.

"Water!" Sonny tore two boards off the first cistern. It was dry. Disappointed, he closed it and followed the hose from cistern to cistern. When he reached the last one, two feet of water sparkled in the bottom. He slid three boards over, jumped in, and pulled them back again. Lying face up in the water, he drank deeply as it flooded over.

Eternity seemed to pass before a shotgun crack shattered the stillness.

"Been here!" called a rough voice.

Sonny heard the men padding around the cisterns and banging the cedar boards, and clenched his fists as they came closer. More boards fell.

"Nothin'," said one. "No nigra. No water neither. Git the dogs!"

"Run to water, but won't find none," said the other. "He'll never git to no water lessen he come to Naked Creek, an' he don't know how to git there for sure. Chances are he took the fire trail yonder—"

"—in the open," interrupted the first one. "Smack-on!"

They cackled again.

Silence followed. Then the crash of a bottle against a cistern.

"Git ourself a little sport!"

Sonny heard spongy footfalls on the needle cover, and the trampling of dry brush as the men climbed out of the gully. One began whistling "Tenting Tonight," the undergrowth smothering the tune as they moved off. Sonny lay still, wondering if he should wait for nightfall. But when the hawk screed, he somehow knew he was safe.

Raising one board, he stood and let the water drip from his overalls. The board fell over with a thud as he peered out like a chick breaking from its shell and searched around twice until certain the Tutwilers had gone. Gaining foothold on a rock inside, he boosted himself over the edge.

Sonny could see the structures of a power line and figured they marked the fire lane. In the opposite direction, he looked where the hemlocks grew thickest and would provide the best cover. Still dripping, he made his way out of the gully and deep into the forest.

For a while he felt cold, even though the air bore down hot and humid, but, before long, breaking through networks of dead limbs, he began to sweat again. He reached a stand of tupelos that blended into a northern oak grove, where deer had cleared paths. Traveling became easier. Checking the position of the sun, he found he was still going north.

Breaking into a clearing, Sonny paused to make sure it was safe. From behind a low-lying limb, he caught sight of a flock of orioles, whistling and feeding on rotting fruit and jumping from bush to bush, flashing color. Two took to the leaders of trees on the opposite side and sang in a regular pattern.

Then a sudden higher pitch, and the orioles flew up in an orange and black whirl and disappeared. Whatever they had sensed, Sonny had not, and he marched out boldly when he saw a gnarled apple tree halfway across. Farther along stood a smaller one. Hunger pushed him to them.

"Don't believe it!" he said. "A Smokehouse apple like I never seen since I's a youngster."

Picking two overripe Smokehouse and putting them into his pockets, he hurried over to the other tree and admired its few remaining apples—green with a pink circle on the sunny side.

"An' a Maiden Blush! Must've been a fine orchard here somedays."

He pulled a decaying Maiden Blush and ate it as he made his way across the clearing and around a copse of trees to another long clearing, stretching toward the northwest. He fled on through the day and evening, skirting once-cultivated fields and abandoned shingler homesteads, keeping cover in the woods when he could and only warily crossing into open ground.

As night approached, Sonny came upon a bittersweet-covered cabin with the chinking all but gone. Half the roof remained; half had fallen against a wattle chimney. He guessed it had been home to slaves. He kicked over a thick growth of milkweed by the entrance, sending their silk through the air, gathered together a pile of the stalks, and entered.

"Home," he said and, leaning over, made a bed of the stalks. Taking out the two Smokehouse, he settled in, eating and listening to the sound of crickets and a barred owl. To Sonny in backwoods Tidewater, the night sky had often turned dead black. He had lived far from city lights, but now, covered with a mixture of cloud and smoke, the sky seemed blacker than ever. No moon or stars shone. Sonny thought of the night predators' having no reflections to pick up with their luminous eyes. But he knew they still hunted through the grasses and brush, by the stream banks, through the air, and along the dark limbs of the night. And he slept.

Sonny had lived so long in the sounds of the Great Dismal that he recognized the dogs in his sleep. He jumped to his feet, ears tense in listening. He heard the baying again, almost imperceptible, arcing somewhere out to the south and listened for their tone, their intensity, their distance.

He figured the men had given up on the fire lane and returned home. Before daybreak they must have unkenneled the dogs and tracked through to the cisterns—and now were circling for scent. Without pausing any longer, he ran out of the cabin and through a patch of thistle and dock.

Ahead beyond the unplowed field, Sonny saw a spine of tulip poplars, surviving tall against the invasion of a farm. He ran and shuffled, stepped over a broken wooden fence, and picked his path through the barnyard and outbuilding ruins. The poplars, the tallest trees he knew in Tidewater but for mast pines, loomed ahead, some covered with the dead brown blossoms of spring. Their enormous height nerved his courage, and he ran among them toward the north.

Fleeing for a quarter mile, Sonny fell out of the poplar woods into a dirt road and turned up it toward a stuccoed-log building with a wooden sign, "Naked Creek Baptist Church."

Gothic points topped the church's broken windows and double doors. Backing up to its foundation bubbled a ten-foot square spring. Watercress, showing its light-green underside, covered the surface, and water ran across a muddy ford in front of him into a grove of swamp maples. In the shadows beyond the spring, he caught sight of the hinny, a gutted deer across its back. They had been there before him. He yearned to fall into the spring to cool his body and to drink its chill, slow-flowing water—but, terrified, he splashed ahead past the hinny.

Farther on, a pasture gate opened into an overgrown field that angled up to a low ridge. Sonny struggled up, through more woods, and down into a dry streambed. Exhausted, he climbed yet another slope, this one covered with the remnants of a peach orchard.

Something moved at the top, and the air cooled as it blew over his temples. A black flutter of feathers lifted itself. A glistening red string of flesh dangled from a buzzard's pink head as it labored above a bloody pile that breathed with gleaming beetles and spirals of humming flies. Sonny's throat dried even more, and his legs shook. The hunters had been here, too.

Then the redtail hawk sailed in and down, dipping over the hill. Encouraged, Sonny climbed on with images of the hunters in his mind. Over the peach tree rise, he stopped at the sight of a white-washed brick cottage.

CHAPTER 7

Shadows fell beneath magnolias lining the cottage's gravel walk. Sonny reckoned it almost noon. Calmed by their shade, he advanced slowly. The path split to the right into a passageway through thick rosebushes, a few white petals still attached, and he followed it around to a square porch at the back.

The walk extended past the porch and circled at a whitewashed stable. Sonny stepped off the gravel onto the quiet of deep grass and headed toward it. In the circle glossy-leafed camellias and dozens of edged-about petunias spoke welcome. Beyond, another bed towered with silver-gray yuccas.

The sun shone hot on his face, but a breeze sifted out of the dogwood-skirted woods behind the stable. Sunlight poured onto the back entryway, covered by white autumn clematis intertwined with grapevines, dripping with hard black grapes. The stairs were well swept, and the windows sparkled

Sonny started when a thin white woman opened the screen door and briskly stepped onto the stoop. She broke a smile and walked toward him.

"'Lo!" she called, offering her hand.

She wore a sheer white dress with blue flowers and a starched cotton-and-lace collar. Her silver hair collected into a bun, denim-blue eyes contrasting attractively. Her skin, youthful; her face, pleasant. He could not judge her age.

Sonny knew she could sense his sizing her up as she stepped down, still holding her hand out. He kept his arms to his sides.

"Hello...ma'am!" he said.

"Somethin' I kin do for you?"

He glanced up at the house.

"Beautiful home, ma'am."

"Why, thank you," she answered. "Well, what you want?"

He felt the heat in his parched body.

"Jis' somethin'..." he said.

"Yes?"

"...somethin' to drink?"

"That's all?"

"Ma'am."

"Hungry a'tall?"

"I'm goin' north."

"You come on in anyways," she said without a hint of suspicion. "You come on."

Sonny did not answer, but took two steps toward her as she turned to climb the steps and open the screen door. She looked back and offered him the door. Putting his fingertips together for a moment, he took three large strides and grabbed it.

A scrubbed oak table lit by a ceiling bulb stood in the middle of the kitchen. White glass-fronted cupboards lined two walls. A green pump craned over an enamel sink, and worn sheet linoleum patterned the floor with morning glories.

"See?" she said, "I'm alone, but I don't fear nobody."

"Yes, ma'am," Sonny answered.

"Always make too much, an' with all these animals runnin' from the fire, hardly have time to eat I'm so interested to see 'em."

She pulled out a chair with a pressed-wood seat from beside an enameled kerosene stove and stood behind it.

"Seen the fire yourself?" she said.

"Ma'am."

"Well, then. Set yourself down." She pointed to the chair seat. "Set yourself."

Sonny hesitated, running a thumb over his crablike yellow fingernails.

"Ma'am?" Sonny said.

"Yes?"

"I'm 'Sonny.'"

"Glad to meet you, Mr. Sonny," she answered. "I'm called 'Maisie.'"

"How do, Miz Maisie!" he said and gingerly offered his hand.

She shook it with a firm grip.

"How do, Sonny!"

His frame relaxed into the chair, and he felt Maisie's trust as she fetched a glass and filled it from the pump. Sonny drank the cold water in one draught.

"Another, ma'am?" he asked.

"Free, ain't it?"

"Ma'am."

"Somethin' to eat?"

"Ma'am."

In minutes Maisie had the stove hot and was frying country ham and eggs and heating coffee, grits, and sausage-pudding. She slid an empty plate and cottage cheese, beaten biscuits, beefsteak tomatoes, and jugs of milk and cream onto the table. The hot items followed. Sonny looked at the food in astonishment.

"Well, git on with it!" Maisie said.

"Ma'am."

Sonny ate deliberately, but not cautiously, appreciating the look of the spread as much as its flavor. He had not eaten such a meal for years. It seemed as much a work of art as the sight of a whiskered catfish in the creek or the waving of yellow eelgrass in a winter wind.

"Where you from?" Maisie said as she wiped her hands on a dishtowel and wrapped it around a chair finial. "Where you say you're goin'?"

"Goin' north."

"North?"

"Ma'am."

"Where to, north?"

Sonny chewed on a piece of salt ham and looked out the door.

"To my papa."

"To your papa!" Maisie exclaimed. "Ain't that grand!" She paused for a moment. "I thought you was runnin' away from the fire."

"Ma'am."

Maisie gazed into his eyes and down at his overalls, and, without any shock, said, "Sonny, you're soakin' wet, an' you're bleedin'." She stared down at his bib. "Want to say, how come?"

Drenched in the cistern, the blood had largely washed out of the overalls and dissipated in the wetness as he traveled along. Body salt had caused the wound to clot, but as he leaned over to eat, the wound opened, and a sharp redness penetrated the bib's pink stain.

"Ma'am?" Sonny answered.

"Want to say, how come?" she repeated.

With a biscuit half, he pushed together the juices and oils on his plate. He was alarmed for a moment, and then the trust returned.

"Been shot."

"Glory!" Maisie said. "An' I here watchin' you bleed. I nursed many a wound in my day, an' I 'spec' some of 'em was on colored folk, too. Let's see." She pointed at his side.

Sonny chewed what was left in his mouth, but held a hand to his bib.

"Git you in no trouble."

"Hah!" she said. "You think cleanin' up a wound's a trouble to me? No, sir, been there an' back. Now—" She reached forward, in one motion unhooked the torn and bloody bib and yanked up his shirt to expose the small wound on his side. "Come in an' I 'spec' went right on through." She smoothed her hand around to his back and found a slightly larger hole. "Right through's a mercy."

Not finding Maisie's search forward or surprising, Sonny accepted it, picturing the in-and-out of the shot. It was what he might have done himself for a wounded deer.

"You know what I'm gonna do, Sonny?" she said. "I'm gonna git you into the tub, an' you're gonna wash yourself, an' you're gonna dump my own peach brandy on these holes, an' I'm gonna wash these clothes an' dry 'em while we got the hot sun. That's it."

Sonny seldom paid attention to anything the game warden told him. Lumpkin, too, was white and from a different world, and Sonny never felt what the warden said had much use to him. But there was a different spirit about Maisie, and he allowed for her care. Before long he immersed himself, knees sticking out, in a massive iron tub on tarnished-gold lions' feet. Maisie toiled above the kitchen sink, overflowing with Ivory Snow bubbles.

A frenzied baying of hounds and a thumping on the kitchen-door glass startled him. He heard Maisie walking toward the door and the crisp closing of a shotgun breach.

"'Day, Maisie!"

"'Day yourself, boys!" she answered sternly. "You're not welcome to my home, neither of you."

"Maisie, we're after a thief come 'cross our farm."

"Yes?"

"A nigra."

The hounds began yipping wildly.

"Might do you a might of harm, you alone."

"Live alone, an' don't take in nobody, least of all the two of you."

"Dogs say he's about."

"Your dogs cain't tell the difference 'tween a shoat an' a sow, they's so dumb!" Maisie shouted.

"What say we track right through your land? You cain't do nothin'."

"Track all you want, but if'n you bother so much as one leaf of my camellias, I'll have the sheriff down to your farm 'fore you kin whistle 'Dixie.'"

"If'n we don't find this nigra, be back to see how he kilt you. You're a stupid ole woman, Maisie. Put up with crim'nals runnin' around an' you don't care."

"I cares about what I cares about," she said and slammed the door on them.

Except for his curly, matted head and one shiny arm, Sonny lay sunken and still beneath the warm water and contemplated the washcloth in his hand and the Mason jar of brandy on the washstand.

CHAPTER 8

Sonny was less frightened by the Tutwilers than bewildered by Maisie. He had come to understood enemies. He understood hunting. He knew what it meant to go to covert. But a white woman's cooking, the nursing of her hands, their laundering of his clothes—these reminded of his own supple care for swamp creatures. He was surprised to find it here.

Clean and refreshed, he rose in the tub, reaching for a flowered towel. He cherished its nap with his fingertips, running his nails between the rows of terry loops. Not knowing how to empty the tub, he stepped out and dried, patting the small holes in his side and back. He lifted the brandy jar from the washstand, unscrewed the metal lid, and dribbled a small amount into the cup of his right hand. He rubbed the brandy gently into each wound, its alcohol stinging only slightly and its thick bouquet invading the air.

Sonny stood for a moment in the middle of the room, wondering what to do next, when he heard the screen door open and close. He was in some sort of pantry, converted into a bathroom. Varnished battens and boards covered the walls, and heart pine the floor. A bulb with a wavy glass shade like an inverted dessert bowl hung from above and trailed an oily string. The fixtures sat around the room like museum pieces, and yellow cottage curtains hung at the window.

"Bathrobe's on the back of the door!" Maisie called from outside the curtains where she stretched his clothing across the camellias and set his sneakers toe-up against the foundation.

"Band-aids in the pocket."

Sonny spotted a pink chenille robe on a roofing nail on the door, searched for the band-aids, found them, and carefully covered each wound. Then he pulled the robe over his tall frame, pleased to find it fit well enough, and returned to the kitchen as Maisie entered from the rear door. She headed toward the chair to dry her hands again on the dishtowel.

"Well, then," she said, "you're lookin' a lot better. Like something out of a Sears catalog."

Sonny beamed in his unaccustomed stylishness. "Sure 'nough," he answered, but immediately knit his brow. "Miz Maisie?"

"'Maisie.'"

"I'm real happy with 'Miz.'"

"All right, then."

"Wants to ask you…"

"Ask."

Sonny's feet slid awkwardly to his chair. He thought a moment before sitting, then pulled the chair out, and sat, curling his hands together in his lap. He scrutinized the oak grain and began running his fingers along the table edge.

"Miz Maisie?" he tried again. "Haven't known hardly nobody for a long time."

"In the deep woods, you mean?" Maisie asked.

"Never thought nobody want to know me," he continued. "Maybe didn't want to know them."

"Well."

"Jis' wants to ask you why you so kind to me."

Maisie threw her hands in the air, bringing them down on the table and laughing. "An' what should I be?" she said.

Sonny hesitated as he felt the table's grain.

"Don't understand," he said.

Maisie turned her face to the door. When she looked back at him, Sonny stared, feeling a bone-deep goodness in her.

"Well, I'll tell you a story—" she said, "if'n you got the time."

Sonny waited. So Maisie began.

"Don't belong down here in Tidewater, any more than the Tutwilers do. We come from whole different parts, an' we got here whole different ways—me through a war, them through orneriness. Strange to say, we're Pennsylvania Dutch.

"I'm an Armentrout Armentrout. I mean Momma was Armentrout, an' Daddy was Armentrout, an' they married, an' she become an Armentrout Armentrout.

"They was peaceable people, being Brethren, an' before I's born, they lived at Possum Hollow by Middle River in the western valley 'cuz my granddaddy an' grandmamma come to settle there. When Stonewall Jackson rode in one day an' tole 'em the Yankees was acomin', Daddy wouldn't take up no arms at first. Didn't believe in it.

"My momma and daddy hid nigras that come their way—an' whites, too. Hid 'em in a grotto up the foothill behind the farm an' covered the entrance with a deadfall. Became a station on the Underground Railroad the Brethren was arunnin'.

"Well, that little farm wasn't worth nothin', but 'twas home to our family, an' with the garden an' the hogs an' cows, my folks an' my brothers an' sisters was mighty happy. 'Til the Yanks come.

"The farm passed sides five times during the war—five times—before my daddy changed his mind—though Momma bloated mighty pregnant with me. He argued with the churchmen, but it didn't make no never mind to him 'cuz he's mad, an' he went right off to fight in the Wilderness. Lay wounded a whole day an' night in the burnin' battlefield an' died. About then Momma heard the Yankees was acomin' back again. Month I was born, I reckon. Don't have no recollection.

"She tole me she took the hams over the hill an' buried 'em. All she had. When the soldiers broke in the door, an' the children hid in the corner, she picked up a broom jis' like a man an' yelled at 'em, 'Git outta here, or I'll beat'—no, Momma didn't say, 'beat your brains out,'—she say, 'or I'll *cut* your brains out! We're peaceable folk!' So they burned down the house an' barn an' left."

Sonny listened without shifting his eyes from the table except for an occasional peep up at Maisie when her voice grew urgent. In his own mind raged the memory of suffering and flight.

"She took the children to live in the cave an' almost missed the deserter who come with Daddy over his horse all covered with flies. Didn't know he was dead, an' when the deserter said, 'Where you want your man?' she never cried nor nothin' 'cuz she knew he was in heaven, so large was her faith. The neighbors dug a hole in the side of the hill, an' the little ones all by themself had to fill it up agin on top of Daddy with no coffin an' no sheet even over 'im."

Sonny shifted his weight and eyed an apple pie by the sink. Maisie caught the glance and jumped up to get it. "Why, of course!" she said. She quickly served big slices and settled down to her story again.

"Deserter was Yankee—kin you believe it? Became my stepfather. Zwichli was his name, a Swiss Sabbatarian, but my momma didn't mind at all since they was peaceable people, too. That's why he deserted an' why he did us a kindness to bring Daddy home. They rebuilt the farm agin, an' the armies never come back."

Maisie looked down as she went on.

"Not even twelve years ole, Daddy Zwichli marry me off to a man come through on a green Studebaker wagon drawn by a real handsome chestnut. Promised to take care of me in Tidewater—didn't say in no swamp. Hubbard James, he was. No religious man, but he said he'd allow us to git married in the wagon right in front of the Brethren church in Mt. Sidney, an' so we did, an' I become Maisie Armentrout Armentrout Zwichli James."

Absorbed by the story, Sonny savored each flake of short crust and each sweet apple slice.

"Not much more to say. Made me stay in the back of the wagon day an' night 'til he pulled in here deep in the Great Dismal to this very house. 'Twas a dream to me, though, 'til I found out there wasn't no church, an' I was his white-girl slave.

"Went off on his wagon week after week an' tole me what to plant an' what to clean an' what to haul an' what to paint. If'n I didn't by the time he got back, he beat me 'til I's half dead.

"Then I found his still on a little island in Cypress Swamp, an' I knowed he was makin' pretty good money. How else could he afford that Studebaker wagon?"

Maisie laughed.

"The last time Hubbard come home, the horse jis' followed the road, he was so drunk. Fell off the seat in the dark, picked up his gun, an' fired at the house. When I come arunnin', he shouts, 'Bear!' an' shot at me—that's all, jis' 'Bear!' Two days later, drunk his own brew down to Lake Drummond an' died of its poison."

Gazing at the bulb, Maisie stopped for breath, then resumed.

"First, I didn't know what to do, but I well knew how to take care of every-thing here sure enough. He made me—'cept for the still. I thought, 'Well, being here's better than being somewheres else, an' who's gonna bother me here?' So I stayed.

"Lord proved it right 'cuz very next month was awashin' out the spring house, an' there in a big ole butter crock was Hubbard's money—old silver an' some gold, not paper, an' with my work here an' what I done with the money, I've lived a good life for what you might call a 'peaceable slave.'"

Then she stopped. They sat in silence, and Maisie began clearing the table. She paused at the sink and twisted to look Sonny full in the face.

"An' what about you?" she said.

Sonny, still deep in the tale of Maisie and Hubbard and the Armentrouts, was taken off guard. He thought about the question while he smoothed both hands down the robe collars.

"Maybe why I'm agoin' north," he answered.

"Why's that?"

"Cuz I don't remember much, I guess. The swamp an' such. An'—"

"That's all?"

Sonny searched for a history like Maisie's, but could not find it, only a dim longness, a oneness of time, everything together.

"Well, how you know where to go?" Maisie asked.

"Remembered I's from Churchland, from near on Portsmouth."

"Wouldn't think of goin' up that way no more," she said. "Besides it's all acomin' down here, not jis' the people, the houses, too."

Sonny could not comprehend that. He thought he knew that peanut and soybean fields stretched out not far ahead. He meant to reach them soon, and then go on to his father's, or where his father used to be. Something inside would keep him walking, no matter what lay out there.

Weariness drifted down on him as the afternoon declined into long shad-ows. He smelled swamp smoke wafting through the house and hoped the fire had not flared nearby. And he yearned for rest.

"Sleep in the barn?" he asked.

"No, indeed!" Maisie said, breaking the stupor. "You'll sleep right here." She pointed to a short hall running to the front stairs. "An' first you'll eat agin, too—oh, my goodness!" she interrupted herself. "Forgot your clothes an' the dew's acomin' on." She hastened out to the camellias.

Maisie soon had the stove going. Flour, meat, jars, and vegetables appeared out of nowhere, but despite the clatter, Sonny nodded off.

"Po' thing," Maisie said to herself, as she arranged his clothes on a chair in front of the stove.

The smell of fried ham with red-eye gravy, boiled okra, and greens with ham essence revived Sonny as Maisie placed a laden blue-willow plate and a large glass of iced tea before him.

"Here 'tis!"

In less than a half-hour Sonny, covered with a soft sheet, stretched out on a bed upstairs, still wearing Maisie's robe. The night sounds that had invaded his shack by the creek sang softly in his mind like a lullaby.

Sometime during the early morning, Maisie rose in her long cotton nightgown and walked stealthily to his door. Pushing it open, she watched the barrel chest slowly rising and falling. She moved to the bedside and placed a thin hand on his gray curls. She rested it there, feeling their rough texture.

"Po' thing," she said again and wondered if the flames would mount and move on her. Then she sighed and withdrew.

"If'n I know they won't, they won't," she announced with conviction and went back to bed.

CHAPTER 9

"What about the Tutwilers?" Sonny asked at the kitchen table, neat as a toddler in his washed overalls.

"Knowed it'd come back to that," Maisie answered.

Finishing a breakfast as varied as the morning before, they drank coffee from large cups and watched chickadees swarm sunflower heads outside the window. The smoke had blown off, and clouds wrapped the sky, promising a pleasant travel day.

"Wouldn't think there was plain folk here in Tidewater. These parts was royally minded. Knowed the mother right well—Resolve—lot younger than the ole man. We was the only two women around here, an' we'd can together sometimes an' pick, or share what we had too much of. Had a gimpy leg, but she'd come right on all the way through them woods an' fields, carrying a basket of green tomatoes would've been hard for a man."

Sonny got up, took their empty cups, and went to the stove.

"Didn't have no other friends, you see. Nobody much about. Nobody come to visit. At first, Momma'd write, but she died not long after Hubbard take me here. Papa Zwichli's glad to git rid of me, so he don't write none. 'Twas Resolve an' me.

"One day I met her down to Naked Creek fetchin' spring water—said it reminded her of the water up to Ephrata in Pennsylvania, where she'd lived. She had some kind of leather buckets, but weren't no lighter than milkin' buckets to my mind. Put a pole between 'em an' carry 'em along home that-away. Anyway, she tole me the Tutwilers was hateful folks, hateful men. All of 'em. Husband'd beat her, an' the boys'd beat her, too. Kin you imagine?

"I say, 'Hateful?' She tole me the ole man had been shunned by the Amish folk 'cuz he'd killed somebody, an' he took her up with Harvey an' Hal an' ran down to Baltimore an' found a job with a shingle company by Fells Point—brought 'em from the Chuckatuck to the James up the Bay.

"Ole man got the idea to take the packet south to Norfolk an' start his own shingle business. Settled that land way over there 'cuz nobody else claimed it. Then he worked 'em like slaves, Resolve an' the boys. Jis' like my Hubbard—if'n they didn't split enough shingle, he beat 'em all, an' then the boys would turn around an' beat her all over agin."

They were well into their second round of coffee before Sonny said anything. He held his cup in both hands, watching the chickadees again.

"More misery in this world than I know of. People jis' carryin' it."

Maisie stared into her cup, "That's not the end."

She'd stopped drinking as tears came to her eyes.

"I had too many black walnuts one year—they're everywhere here—an' Resolve knew jis' how to git 'em out by halves. Never seen nobody could git 'em out like that. So I husked 'em an' took quite a bag over to her.

"When I came on to the back of the house, I heard nailin' to the front an' went around to the yard. There was Harvey an' Hal makin' two cedar coffins jis' as happy—one for the ole man—an' one for Resolve—bloody as kin be, all lyin' there. Boys tole me they'd killed 'em both. Hated 'em both an' killed 'em both with an ax."

"Kilt 'em!" Sonny said, his head jerking upward.

"Oh, po' Resolve!" Maisie said.

She sighed a long, heavy sigh and watched the chickadees for a moment.

"Knowed I was next if'n I said somethin', but they must've had enough killin' for a time."

She looked back at the rim of her cup.

"All these years, an' we come to a standstill. They's afraid I'd tell, I reckon, an' I's afraid they'd kill me dead. But nobody ask too many questions down here. So we been at standstill since I don't know when. Even got over my fear.

Harvey an' Hal ignore me, an' I ignore them all this time. But in a way it's been some comfort to know Resolve's still lying there, about my only friend."

Nothing was said for a while—Maisie having made peace for herself, and Sonny on his way to finding it, driven by fire and his own memories and something else.

"Maisie," Sonny said finally, "I got to go 'fore the day's far along."

"I know. Send you with somethin' keep you on your way."

She got up, rooted through the icebox and a cupboard, and packed food in two brown paper bags.

"Take care of you for a while," she said, offering them to Sonny.

On his way back to the dirt track, which Maisie had told him would become a road, then a blacktop, Sonny paused and waved to her with the lunch bags, pleased to return to his mission.

"Find the Portsmouth Ditch, an' it'll git you to Portsmouth!" she called. She gazed at him with the look of a friend who had long been without companionship, but not clinging—the look of one who knew to trust whatever had brought them together had to be appeased by their separation.

In a few hours, as Sonny emerged from a soft-timber wood, the sky exploded into cornflower blue, the sun jangling in the middle. No smoke in the westerly breeze. No black cloud buffered the eastern horizon. He crossed through deserted tobacco and cotton fields, now owned by the government, pulsating with Black-Eyed Susans and chicory.

He spotted two or three rabbits. White-tailed deer flagged him, only to check themselves on lush grass a hundred feet away. Mockingbirds worked bittersweet, winterberry, and holly berries into their gullets like snakes swallowing rats. Sparrows and mice trailed over the ground, searching for seeds. No-seeums, bees, and flies gave dimension to the air around him, preparing to tunnel for the winter.

Sonny was confident he would prove Maisie wrong. He would find peanuts and soybeans as soon as he crossed the invisible line between public and private land. The endless flat fields would be harvested, but he would recognize the round peanut leaves, even dried and lying in the dirt. The farmers could not have gotten them all.

Before he ranged much farther, a thundering to his right stopped him in midstep. Flashing on the horizon, flights of Navy fighters in groups of four began rumbling in from the east, flying low and moving off toward the west. Their roar vibrated the ground under his feet. Wildlife froze.

On and on came the plane packs, fleeing the eastern smoke—planes Sonny had seen many times before—squadrons of fighters, then bombers, then transports and squat aircraft, piggybacked by radar hats—all evacuating the coastal bases, tracing contrails over each other.

He stood in wonder as the sky glittered in loud metal, so loud that his bones shook. When the planes finally disappeared as quickly as they had come, he could not reckon how long they had taken to pass, so enthralling had been the assault. Then the earth echoed with silence.

"Peace in the valley," Sonny said to himself. Enjoying the stillness for a moment, he walked on.

The late afternoon waxed warm. He came upon a decaying tobacco barn crowded by a weeping willow and a short butternut. Entering through a rotted door, he thought to spend the night, but he had hours of daylight left, so he settled into its slatted shade to eat a late lunch. Maisie had not spared anything: buttered biscuits, a quince, fried ham slices, chicken legs, and three green tomatoes, all wrapped in wax paper.

Sonny attacked the ham between two biscuits, tearing the tough slice with broken teeth and picking crumbs off his bib. He ate as if at a banquet, deliberately chewing each nutty bite, remembering Maisie's oak table and slipping his thumb and fingers over both sides of the wax paper. When he had eaten the meat and biscuits, he lay back on the dirt floor, packed with years of leaf scrap, and savored the aroma of earth and tobacco and ham. He gazed at the rafters where frayed strings and shredded leaf shards still hung.

"How long since my people cut these fields?" he wondered aloud. As a boy he had known a slave, old and infirm, sitting in some cabin of the remote past like this one.

Sonny slaked his thirst with the largest tomato and ate half the sour, fibrous quince for dessert. Tomatoes did not grow near the creek, but he often picked one from a volunteer when roving out toward civilization. He had found a quince bush by a shucker's shack once and returned to it through the years until it died.

Packing what remained of his food, Sonny decided to cover more miles before night. He turned onto all fours, hoisted himself to his feet by grabbing a splintered hand-hewn doorpost, holding a paper bag as he rose. Looking out across the countryside, he felt energized and stepped into the declining afternoon.

"I'm acomin', Papa," he said.

And off he went into the sounds of approaching evening—sharp peeper chirps, the mellow sawing of crickets, and intermittent hoots of a horned owl, all broken by a blackbird squabble behind him. A breeze pushed in from the west, bearing the sun's lingering warmth.

For an hour he walked through more cotton and tobacco fields as he had half the day—until he came upon a change in the terrain. It had been plowed recently and meant a different kind of farming, one allowed for a few years after the swamp became public.

"Peanuts for sure!"

In the dusk Sonny spied a regular row of cedars. Their pattern told him they marked a creek and might be the boundary of a worked field beyond. He hurried his pace through saplings and dying weeds, keeping his eyes on the line, anticipating what might be waiting.

He stopped when the redtail swept out of the evening sky like the return of a jet fighter. It poised in midair, rotored in a point, then fluttered back and forth from left to right and back, as it had done three days before—screeing all the time in a dismay Sonny had not heard in all his wilderness years.

"Flushing out prey?" he called. But the hawk seemed to Sonny to be threatening like a kitten puffing up before a hungry hound.

CHAPTER 10

Sonny watched the redtail as it dove toward him, but night drew on, and he wanted to get to the creek and the field he hoped lay beyond. He continued down an incline when the hawk brushed his hair with its wing and disappeared.

Night sounds diminished, and a full moon vied with the setting sun. At the slope's moist bottom, wild grasses grew tall, painting dewdrops below the knees of his overalls. Straining to see where to cut into the cedars and ford the creek, Sonny caught movement in the thickness and knew deer would be emerging from cover to drink in the sanctuary of night. Then he stepped among the black cedars.

It came with no notice, a fierce blow. And another. Sonny tumbled over, blood running from his crown into his eyes and onto his overalls. Stunned, he heard voices above, shouting and cackling. Painfully he bent his thick neck to glimpse men jumping and waving their arms.

"Whee-oh!" one shouted. "The nigra brought *dow*-en!"

Panic enveloped him as he recognized Harvey and Hal Tutwiler. They had strayed too near civilization to shoot, and dogs would have given them away.

"Thought you got away," the other one yelled and took another whack. "Thought we couldn't find you. Thought the ole lady'd protect you. Got to know, nigra, we ain't live in these parts for nothin'. We knows the land like nobody!"

They swung gunstocks around their heads like baseball bats. They struck him hard in the kidneys. The pain was so severe that Sonny grunted like air escaping a thick balloon. He tried to crawl when the stocks struck his legs.

"Why?" he asked.

The Tutwilers cackled again.

"'Why?'" Harvey answered, leaning toward Sonny's bloody ear. "'Cuz—jis' 'cuz. Jis' 'cuz you gits where you don't belong."

Hal fell in, "How we know what you done to the ole lady, what you took from 'er? How we know what she *tole* you?"

"I didn't—" Sonny started.

"An' you is sport, man. You's sport," Hal crowed.

Sonny no longer tried to understand. He lay like a pig to slaughter as they whooped up into the pewter moonlight. Prostrate, he saw one pale star and fell unconscious.

Night brooded on. Insects settled into hidden places, and night hunters slid noiselessly through the underbrush. An owl swept high into a sycamore. Deer passed by the sandy creek bank, grazing, drinking, off guard.

In the peaceful cedar grove the black man lay on his side, legs splayed as if kicking a ball, arms in front, muscled wrists limp as a ballerina's. Blood seeped into the sand. A red fox sneaked close to smell it, lifted its nose toward Sonny's face, and backed off into the grass. Deer hooves grated in the quartz granules.

His hand twitched. One foot dragged sideways.

"Papa?"

An hour later, he moaned and opened his eyes, crazing blood-caked eyelids. The middle of the night, and he thought he might be dead. The sand felt cold. He scooped it into his palm. Indeed, coldness—rough and real to his fingers.

He was alive, but lay still, not certain whether to play opossum against the return of the Tutwilers or to escape upstream. A doe caught his movement, watched, then sauntered off downcreek, winding among the cedars in search of greens. Clouds moved over the moon, leaving the landscape blacker than ever.

Supporting himself on an elbow, Sonny sat up, and his body thumped with blood, rushing to the wounds and bruises. To his surprise, strings of lights loomed across the horizon beyond the stream. Like a weir in a tidal river, they ran the breadth and depth of the distance—as far as he could see—shining on row upon row of houses.

Yellow lamps flickered in the windows. Rooms flashed from shadow to light, vibrating in varied shades of electric blue and pink. Car beams pierced toward him, bent away, reappeared. Motor hum and the press of tire on concrete fluxed across the creek.

"Maisie's right!" he exclaimed. What he saw hurt more than the beating. "It's all come right to here. They ain't no peanuts!"

Sonny had wanted to return to a world known decades before, but now he saw that that world was not there, had not been for a long time. And, if that world was not here, what about Papa? With the final fear, he lapsed back into unconsciousness, sinking onto the sand like a drunkard on a park bench. The night drew on.

When he came to, he sensed fluttering by his head. The redtail landed and preened itself at the creek's edge, spreading one tawny wing and grooming it like a cat. It flapped to get the water out, fanning its rusty tail. Unmindful of Sonny, it rose effortlessly into the air, and Sonny heard the muffled wings beat into the darkness.

He rose and staggered to the watercourse, where he knelt to wash his hands and face, flinching as he rubbed water into the wounds. Rinsing, he began to feel life in him again. He looked around for bedding and hobbled among the cedars to a woodland cul-de-sac that held a cache of fallen leaves. He stooped down and rolled onto his back as pain streaked through his body. He could endure it. He could not endure the growing conviction that his quest was in vain.

His mind wandered over the sunny savanna he had fled, through the piney woods, along his creek, onto the pier. Was all that gone, too—burned, desolate? Would the creatures return? And Lumpkin? Had he escaped? And the shack?

As he lay in the blackness, a lullaby from his childhood crept in. He hummed as the words returned:

> Softly the sta-ars was ashine-in',
> Shinin' with gol-ol-d'n ray.
> Over the bay-ay-bee Jes-us,
> Cradled up-on-on the hay.

Softly the bay-abe was asleep-in',
Angels their wa-atch was akeep-in',
Calm an' secure, tender an' pu-re
Jesus, the holy chile.

And he fell asleep.

CHAPTER 11

"You all right?"

A hand touched Sonny on his blood-splotched shoulder as sunlight struck through the cedar sprigs.

"You all right?" the voice repeated.

Sonny stirred and strained to open his eyes.

Lozenge-like black eyes set in a gaunt face gazed down from a teenager's six-foot height. He wore jeans and a khaki turtleneck. He had an earring in his left ear, and a rubber band held his brown hair in a ponytail. A yellow Labrador, not much more than a puppy, sat by his right hiking shoe, excited at what it had found.

Groggy, Sonny was unsure whether he felt all right or not.

"Me and Tugboat, we come along here mornings," the boy said. "You all right?"

Sonny pushed up onto one elbow.

"Don't know," he answered in a whisper, looking up at the teenager. "Who you? Where you from?"

"Nowhere," the boy answered with a chuckle.

"I mean...where you live?"

"Over there." He pointed toward the line of townhouses.

Sonny sat up painfully and gazed at where the lights had been the night before. "It's a big house."

"Not all of them. Just the one with the open garage."

The retriever, tongue hanging out, whined.

"Hush, Tugboat!" the boy commanded. He grabbed the dog by the shoulders, turned it around toward the field behind, and shouted, "Squirrel!" The retriever lit out.

"But…you all right?" the boy said again, focusing on Sonny, who was raising himself carefully onto his knees. Then, tottering, he tried to get a foot under. The teenager took his forearm to pull him up.

"Thinks I am," Sonny answered, steadying himself.

The boy put out a hand. "Hans."

Sonny studied him, then offered his hand. "Sonny," he said quietly. Hans shook it hard.

"Somebody been on you?" Without waiting for an answer, he went on. "Come on get something to eat."

"Got plenty of food," Sonny said, searching for his brown bag. Not finding it, he mumbled, "Used to."

Tugboat returned in a tumble and pawed at Sonny, who took the dog's silky head in his big hands and scratched behind its ears, rotating the head right and left. The motion caused Sonny to wince, but he smiled through it.

"Guess I needs somethin'," he said.

"Let's go, then," Hans said, walking backwards out of the cedar copse and gesturing to the dog. "Come, Tugboat, come!"

They meandered away from the stream bank, around a plowed pile of dirt, and along toward the townhouse, the retriever roaming ahead, stirring up mice and ground-feeding birds. When Sonny staggered, the teenager slipped under his arm.

They entered the garage, and Hans led Sonny to a tool room to the left, outfitted as a bedroom—a bed with a Heavy-Metal-stickered headboard on one wall and tan futon across the opposite. Rock star posters decorated the plaster, thick around a stereo-combo like a space command center. A plywood desk sat next to it, mounted with an elaborate computer setup, swimming with multi-colored screen-saver fish.

"My pad," Hans announced, taking off his sweater to reveal a faded Heavy Metal T-shirt. "Folks don't want me upstairs so I duck down and leave 'em alone when they're here, which is never. Guess I wasn't part of their plans. I'm a latch-key kid—or garage-door kid maybe!" He laughed.

"Gone to work?" Sonny asked.

"For the year! Me and Tugboat, we're just livin' here and lookin' after the house and doin' our 'thang.'" Tugboat eyed Hans when it heard its name, then wandered over to an empty bowl on the floor. "All alone 'til I got him, but I'm used to it—as long as the checks keep comin'."

"Git used to it…," Sonny said. "Sometime wished I had somebody."

"Hey, you're shakin', man!" Hans said, seeing Sonny in full light.

He pulled out the desk chair for Sonny, who sat down and stared at the computer with its colored fish gliding over a midnight screen, evolving from magenta to lemon to apricot. The teenager parked himself on the bed's footboard.

Sonny trusted Hans the moment he saw him handle the retriever—a boy from another world, but open, accepting. Hans intrigued him: a teenager happening upon a bloody, old black man in a leaf nest, but not a bit fazed. Inviting him home as if it were an everyday occurrence. The dog had showed more surprise.

"Hans, does you know anythin' called 'Portsmouth Ditch'?"

"Sign few blocks up."

"Says?"

"Want to see?"

"I do." Sonny made a motion to get up.

"Whoa! You're in bad shape. Lie down on that futon—I'll get us some Total or something."

"Total?"

"Cereal."

"I'd like some," Sonny answered, looking around. "The foo-ton?"

"Sofa there—it's a bed." Hans went over and pulled the futon open. "Here."

"Well," Sonny said.

Through the years of change, even though he had never ridden a bus or eaten frozen food or done many things most Americans had, Sonny accepted them all with little curiosity. He knew he came from a different era, had different ways of doing things, respected things many did not. Yet few differences bothered him, except those that bewildered his heart. He knew love. He knew trust. He knew malice, but he did not understand it.

Hans left for the upstairs kitchen, but soon returned with large bowls of cereal and milk. The two ate enthusiastically, the dog poking at the boy's arm as he sat again on the footboard.

"Good's grits," Sonny announced.

"What's grits?" Hans answered.

Sonny looked up. "Well…they're white an' cooked an'—"

"Oh, yeah. Seen 'em at Hardee's. I'd rather have a croissantwich."

Sonny did not respond, happy with the cereal and not knowing who "Hardee" was—not to mention whatever odd food he served, except for grits.

"So what happened?" Hans asked.

"Why you want to know?"

"You all banged up like that."

Sonny chewed. "Got beat on by a couple boys didn't have no sense."

"How come?"

"Jis' wanted somebody to beat on, I guess."

"I know about that," Hans said.

The teenager put his bowl down and smoothed Tugboat's head, stretching and holding its ears back, looking into the dog's eyes.

"You live with somebody?" he asked.

Sonny stopped chewing his last spoonful, "Nah."

"You live alone?"

"Gulls, cranes, 'coons. I got others."

"Like Tug?"

"Yeah, like you got Tugboat."

Sonny set his empty bowl next to him on the futon while Hans still looked into the dog's eyes.

"Lonely at all?" the teenager asked.

Sonny reflected a moment, and the boy darted a glance at him.

"Might be," Sonny answered.

"That's a help!" Hans burst out, pretending irritation.

Sonny beamed. "I want to see my Papa."

"Me, too!"

"Used to live up to Churchland, up toward Portsmouth. That's why I'm agoin' to the Portsmouth Ditch."

"Going to see your father up that way?"

"Hope so."

"*Your* father?" Hans repeated in disbelief, then reconsidering, "Want company?"

Sonny beamed again. "You belongs here with Tugboat."

"What makes you think I couldn't be home somewheres else?" Hans appeared annoyed.

"Could. Not tryin' to put you off or nothin'. Jis' don't think it's now."

Hans scrutinized Sonny's face and pushed the dog away.

"You alone as you thinks," Sonny continued. "I'm from the Great Dismal, an' happy enough there. 'Til the great fire. I made my life there. You made a life here—but you're young. I'm ole. We all gotta git over somethin'."

Hans swaggered from the footboard onto the desk chair. "I *am* alone," he said angrily.

"What's that talkin', an' me sittin' here?" Sonny asked with a laugh. "An' Tugboat?" He looked down at the dog. "Maybe that's why I'm here. Jis' to prove you ain't alone today, then maybe not never. Nothin's impossible."

They talked on for hours, seldom moving from where they sat, working through sandwiches and potato chips and soft drinks, on and on through the noon hour and into the early afternoon. As the day began to lengthen, Sonny got up and walked to the garage door, Tugboat at his heels. He wanted to move on. Finding himself with Hans in a townhouse development might be some important part of being drawn to Papa, but he had to continue.

Late in the afternoon Hans and Tugboat walked him a few blocks to a grass strip beside a concrete slough with spindly trees, snaking through a townhouse wasteland. There from a blue-and-orange Virginia State marker, the boy read out loud:

CHINQUAPIN PARK

This linear park runs for twenty miles
along the site of Portsmouth Ditch,
a former drainage and boat canal from
the Great Dismal Swamp to the Elizabeth River.

"You can follow northeast to Route 17," he said. Then, stooping to snuggle his face in the dog's neck, "It'll wind around a bit, but it'll take you where you're going." He took Sonny's hand. "Will you come back?"

"Might, an' might not. But you don't need me."

Hans hugged Sonny tight, turned, called to the dog, and jogged away, looking back only once.

CHAPTER 12

Sonny forged on with renewed enthusiasm. The townhouses ended in red clay and heaps of chain-dragged trees. Except for the ditch renewal project—a gutter of swamp water—the landscape stretched untouched. Derelict shanties sat among fields of weeds and refuse, and trash trees flourished in impoverished farmyards.

Gnats flew around his eyes, and the farther he walked, the more smoke he smelled even though the air looked clear. Leaf skeletons lay like lace along the way; the air movement of his passing legs shattered ones near the path. A few flew up and slowly settled.

Hiking a mile on a worn path, Sonny came upon a rabbit ranch behind a ramshackle house sitting on cement blocks. Scarlet sumac crowded the hutches. As he approached, squeals tensed his ears: the ranchers were butchering. He went on, excited to reach the highway, and he took comfort in Hans's prediction that there was no way he could miss it.

Before long, buildings appeared. Low houses with peeling trim backed up to the park with dying camellias and azaleas scattered about their yards among bikes and basketball hoops. Children rode plastic tricycles up and down driveways, and mothers hung out laundry. Occasionally, a child ran to its property edge and eyed him. Mothers caught sight of him over kitchen sinks and watched until he shuffled out of sight toward the northeast.

After a while, Sonny came upon an elderly white man in stained jeans, retrieving a rake from an ash-covered shed. He slowed to watch while the gardener cleared a patch of raised beds, piling tomato vines and wilted leaves into a compost heap.

"How do?" the gardener said when he saw Sonny, his face puffy with purple bruises.

"Afternoon!" Sonny answered. "Nice afternoon."

"Want to make some money?"

"Off to Churchland."

"You crazy? Ain't no Churchland," the gardener said, kicking the soil and exploding ash deposits around his feet. "All 'Chesapeake City' now. All city."

Sonny glanced up the trace, not taking in what he had said. "Town's a town. Cain't take that off, can ya?"

"Well, they did, fella. So forgit it."

Sonny wondered how a town could disappear. "Churches still there?" he asked, "The smith?"

"Who got need of a smith?"

"Houses? They still there?"

"People gotta live. People livin' everywhere, nothin' but tearin' down an' buildin' up."

Sonny suddenly found his dream fallen dead—Papa gone for sure—and he dropped down onto the edge of a bed.

"Mind if'n I rest a while?"

The gardener looked sympathetically at Sonny and at his bloodied shirt and overalls. "Set yourself on that bench over to the shed."

Sonny got up and ambled to the side of the garden and, leaning on the makeshift building, carefully lowered himself and inclined against its wall. The sun moved toward setting, and a light air current blew along the ditch. Insect buzzing lapsed into the peeps of frogs.

"Don't know as I kin go on," he said.

"Big man like you wouldn't mind sleepin' in the shed, would ya?"

"Could," Sonny answered.

The man wiped his hands on his jeans and walked back toward the house. "Bring you supper," he said over his shoulder.

Sonny watched as the evening sky reflected in the ditch, a winding red cut piercing the dusk, but no evening birds sang.

"No use," he said and pulled himself up. Alongside the shed stood a stack of boards, which Sonny laid out on the shed's dirt floor and lay down. He thought about Maisie's kindness, Hans's loneliness. Churchland. He had had a goal; the gardener had taken it away. His quest ebbed, and he decided to return to the Dismal, avoiding both the dangers and the joys of his coming. Defeat spread through him, heartbeat-by-heartbeat, and he stared out vacantly at the lights across the park.

After a while, the gardener came around the raised beds. "Supper, fella," he said. "Pot roast an' tatas."

"'Obliged," Sonny said, getting up. "Good of you."

The gardener eyed the board bed Sonny had made for himself. "You'll be comfortable enough…well, goodnight!"

"Yes, suh."

Sonny fell to the meal with gusto. He ate quickly, put the plate aside, and stretched out on the planks, pulling a burlap bag over him. The brutal beating, the long walk, the disappointment had taken their toll, and through the night's first half, he slept like a hibernating bear. Nothing flickered his eyelids or twitched his fingers—just heavy, soundless sleep.

But in the early morning hours, Sonny's mind sparked with violence. The Tutwilers crept up the levee, guns at the ready. Tugboat lay dead among the vines on the raised beds. A crazed Miz Maisie toppled from the shed roof. Hans's parents beat him endlessly with a strop. Flames enveloped the shed, exploding its dry boards. The gardener came to slice Sonny's neck.

Sonny awoke with a jerk and sat right up on the hard boards. Getting to his feet, he listened intently into the night as he had in the swamp, and decided to leave immediately. He would find his way back through the fields and forest and, with any luck, escape the Tutwilers and live off the land until he got home. If the swamp shelter had burned and if the land were all scorched, he knew what he would be dealing with. But if Churchland had disappeared, Papa had disappeared with it. He could no longer return. He stepped over the shed threshold and peeped into a land never quite dark, the sky stained with pink even at night.

Returning to the trail, he faced southwest, but, before proceeding farther, he caught sight of the redtail hawk at the corner of the garden, its yellow eyes reflecting the light of distant street lamps. It was hunching down on a tomato stake, elbow joints poking in Sonny's direction, its beak opening and closing as it emitted an almost inaudible, but ominous, hiss.

"What, friend?" Sonny asked.

The hawk lifted without effort, and sailed toward and above him. He watched it mount overhead, and then proceeded on his way back to the swamp—only to be stopped by the hawk's landing on a fence post ahead, threatening in the same eerie manner. Sonny halted and stared. And then he knew. He turned and walked, first hesitantly, then resolutely, to the northeast.

Moving through the semi-night of early morning, he followed the ditch until he saw filling stations, fast-food joints, and small warehouses just before the ditch disappeared into a culvert. He had reached Route 17. It would take him back to Churchland. That much he remembered.

Sonny climbed the side of the culvert and pulled himself onto the highway shoulder, flinching at the heavy traffic, rumbling along before daybreak—the tankers, car-transports, and vans so different from the battered and rusted cars he had come upon at the swamp margins.

He turned left along the shoulder and walked on, passing a junkyard, an Arby's, a gas station, a mini-mall; and then the sequence seemed to repeat itself mile upon mile. His pace picked up as the pulse of civilization invaded him, and he traveled to its beat. After a few more miles, sunlight broke the upper sky over a bank of cloud and smoke to the east. The traffic roar and the commercial buildings no longer seemed as foreign.

Sonny pushed on for another mile when he heard a familiar regular clatter. The earth began to tremble with a welcome trembling. Grinding toward an underpass in front, Norfolk and Western double-diesel locomotives were dragging coal cars from West Virginia mines to Norfolk wharves. He had seen such trains many times. He knew their tracks led to Churchland.

CHAPTER 13

Where the tracks once passed through swamp and woods, they now ran behind shopping centers and industrial parks. Walking the ties pleased Sonny. They never lay quite right for pacing, so he alternated between stepping and leapfrogging. The irregular walk brought images and sounds of years long gone—hearing the click-clack of endless coal cars, riding a draught horse, staring at penny candy in the confectionary. But with them also came memories of that fearful night he had left.

Slanting across the general road grid, the tracks headed straight toward the edge of Churchland, and he made good progress. Nothing looked familiar, not the cars or businesses, but he hoped that when he got to territory covered as a boy, he would know where he was.

Leaving the development that pushed out of Portsmouth, the tracks cut through clear-cut trees and thicket. A half-mile into it, Sonny spotted a large northern oak sheered off by lightning and burdened with limbs below the break, so heavy they lay on the ground.

"Camp Meetin' Oak!" he exclaimed, glowing, remembering revival nights under its branches. "Must be—Camp Meetin' Oak!"

Breaking through brambles by the tracks, Sonny made his way to the tree, which dropped rusting leaves to a layer of mold below, where few plants grew.

He ducked under its limbs, searching for the old benches, simply made by driving poles into the ground and nailing boards on top. And there they were, not the seats, but the patterned remains of decaying supports. Sonny kicked one.

He loved and hated this place. When he was a boy, it had provided a sanctuary of quiet and strength during his daytime adventures, and he felt the oak a surviving friend. It had also been the site of his greatest anguish.

Leaving the meeting ground, Sonny pressed through the brambles to a road with dead grass down the middle. Mornings and evenings as a youth he had walked this road—folks called it the "horn" because it curved to and from Churchland in an almost perfect semicircle. The horn was bisected by the Norfolk and Western tracks that led from here west to the Nansemond River and Richmond and the mountains, tracks that had once made Sonny dream of other places. Standing at the edge of the horn, he could go in either direction to reach town, follow the tracks to his boyhood home. He decided to walk straight through.

When he turned off the rail bed, the sun blistered, and late-autumn air pumped steamy and sluggish. But he had arrived. Sighing, he surveyed the wide weed lot with bamboo and sumac runs, brilliant in yellow and red, which had been his yard. The house was gone. The sheds and barn were gone. The fruit trees were gone. The outhouse down back was gone. Nothing remained of the coleus that had encircled the whitewashed tree trunks or the broad, high clump of yuccas or the red canna bed in tractor tires out front. Everything gone.

Could I be wrong? Sonny wondered. Had he mistaken the location of the tracks and where they had run along the yard? Had he exaggerated their closeness because the locomotives had loomed so large then?

Walking across the yard, he dragged his feet through a tangle of crabgrass, chicory, and chickweed, leaving a line of crushed vegetation. Halfway across, a toe caught a root, tripping him and tumbling him onto his back. Both arms behind, he pushed up into a sitting position and untangled his foot.

"I'll be!" he said, pulling the root along. "Yucca! It's yucca! It's where the yucca were." Reaching between his feet, he scrabbled in the weed mat, yanking it aside. Yucca plants sprouted beneath.

With new vigor, he dragged his feet again from one remembered planting to the next, searching. A few yards along, he bent to pick up a handful of dried pecans and remembered how a Philadelphia man had admired his father's broad tree, "Don't grow up by us—too cold." Sonny knew stood exactly where the tree had been.

Stuffing the pecans into his pocket, he took five large paces, almost leaping, and started kicking at other weeds until he struck something solid. He dragged up the weed-and-grass net to expose broken concrete beneath.

"The pump!" he said. "Right here were the pump."

He tore the grass farther back to reveal a six-foot-square base with rusted cast-iron collar in the middle. He thought about the times he had primed the pump, the times he had brushed his teeth there with his finger, the times he had carried water to his mother's soapstone sink, the times he had filled the bathtub on the second floor, the floorboards spread with newspaper.

On a summer evening Papa would put his rocker on the front lawn over near the ditch and beyond the pump to catch any air that might pass along the road. Neighbors walked up and down after dinner, sometimes going all the way around the horn. Raising his forearm, Papa would wave and nod his head with a scarcely heard, "How y'all?"

Only one white family had lived in Churchland then, out by the crest of the horn. The Stevenses puzzled the town folk. It didn't make sense to them that somebody would come all the way from Massachusetts, a distant and mysterious land, just to start a goat farm here. But the Stevenses had a sweetness about them that overcame rumors about whites and strangers Sonny sometimes heard.

"Jis' why?" neighbors wondered. "Jis' why'd somebody up an' come to Tidewater from the North jis' like that?" Everybody in town knew everybody else—knew his parents and grandparents and great-grandparents, and sometimes knew who their former masters had been. But the Stevenses seemed good people, and their reason for coming just magnified their intrigue.

They used to let Sonny watch the milking and give him a jar of yellow milk to take home, but he had had one real concern.. It had to do with Honor, a white kid he loved to pet beside the milking shed. The Stevenses never attended to Honor, and one day Sonny asked why.

"Milk the nannies," Mrs. Stevens had said. "Eat the kids."

A month later she appeared at the screen door to Sonny's kitchen and called for him.

"Gotta present for you," she announced, holding out a silky flat bundle.

Sonny took the offering and began to unfold it.

"It's Honor," she said.

Wrapped in memory, Sonny looked off into the remaining trees at the property's boundary. His eyes tracked down their trunks and back along the overgrown grounds. Rotating on his heels, he sought every angle.

It was then that he caught sight of the blacksmith shop.

CHAPTER 14

The smithy sat kitty-corner across Route 17—the forge where his father had shoed horses and repaired farm equipment for more years than Sonny knew. A wooden store with dusty windows leaned against its side. No one had painted it, but it had held up well enough through Tidewater summers and fall hurricanes.

An enamel "Grapette" sign angled in one window, and "Dr. Pepper" in the other, drinks Sonny could seldom afford. Above the forge's sliding doors Sonny made out the familiar advertisement, "Clabber Girl." To their right was nailed a rusted yellow-and-green "John Deere" sign. On the door itself appeared the faded words, "George Lawton, Blacksmith."

Transfixed, Sonny sank onto the grass clump he had pulled from the pump foundation and stared across the intersection. He wondered if Papa still lived and what to say to him if he did. "Supposin' he don't know me? An' if'n he ain't there, who'd remember?"

A mockingbird chased a band of squawking crows through the sun-filled sky. The redtail dashed between them, the crows lighting out for a tulip tree and the mockingbird diving down to camellia skeletons at the end of the yard. The hawk glided over pines, curved back toward Sonny, and then beat toward the smithy, where it landed on the roof and folded its wings like an umbrella.

Sonny heard familiar metallic ringing, one on, one off. One on, one off. He got up, boiling with anticipation, walked over the side road, paused for the cars on Route 17, and started to cross. The ringing repeated until he was halfway over, then a clunk and sizzle.

When he entered the smithy's darkness, the forge pit glowed bright by the anvil. Steam rose from a keg on the dirt floor. His eyes penetrated the cluttered dim space and rested on an old worker, inspecting a pile of metal in the far corner. As he stepped inside, he felt the coal's heat on his face.

Without turning around, the man said, "Been awaitin'."

Sonny hesitated, not knowing what to say.

"Taken a long time," the man continued.

"Been awaitin'?" Sonny answered.

"Been next to you every step of the way."

"How you mean?"

"Think I'd leave you alone?"

Sonny's brow wrinkled. "Who are you?" he asked. "I'm alookin'—"

"Why, I'm your daddy, boy!"

The blacksmith leaned into the pile, pulled out a piece of junk iron with his right hand, and studied it. Smacking it lightly against his opposite palm, he turned around with a broad smile.

"Mighty glad to see you!" he said.

A white handlebar mustache covered Papa's lower face. Shirtless, he wore a leather apron from neck to knee. He held out his arms toward Sonny, the scrap hanging from one hand, and motioned his son toward him. Tears filled Sonny's eyes as he rushed over and embraced him. They clung to each other, the one crying, the other smiling as if he were the sun itself.

"Papa, I'm mighty glad to see you, too. Been so long," Sonny said through his tears.

"Jis' to you," Papa answered. "I been here an' there all the time. But I do loves to have you here now." Sonny wrote Papa's nonsense off to his age.

The smithy broke off the embrace and, holding the scrap out in front of him, guided Sonny over to the bellows. "Pump on that for me, will you?" he said, pointing to a long handle. His muscles aching, Sonny reached up and pulled it down, feeling the resistance of the thick leather accordion. Gradually, he forced it down and up, and flames fingered through the coal. The more he pumped, the hotter the forge pit grew until it turned white, and Papa thrust the metal in.

"Keep apumpin'. This one needs it all," Papa said as he turned the scrap over. The white heat closed around the metal, and when it turned orange, he softly called, "You kin stop now."

He pulled the metal out, placed it on the anvil, and the beat began. One strike on the metal, one on the anvil. He hammered one end into a curve and thrust it into the keg, which exploded with steam. He repeated the process along the length, using tongs to handle the metal, designing as he went.

"Pump on some more," Papa said.

Sonny put himself back into it, working the handle. The coals turned white again, and, after much heating, hammering, and tempering, Papa proudly held up a crude shape.

"What's it for?" Sonny asked.

"Could be a shop sign for makin' people—like makin' shoes—don't you know?" Papa announced with a laugh. "Or whatever else you wants it for."

Sonny marveled that it was, indeed, the outline of a man with his black arms and legs stretched out like a spread eagle.

"Why you make it?"

"We got talkin' to do, you an' me," Papa answered as he led Sonny to the store.

Its lopsided board walls painted moss green, faded and dirty, rose to a high ceiling from which hung a flyspecked milk-glass globe on a corroded chain. A loaded flypaper scroll dangled halfway down.

Long windows let in sunbeams, flying with stirred particles. Dusty National Geographics covered the windowsills, most of the floor, and a worn wooden desk. The only surfaces not piled with magazines and corrugated boxes were a desk chair and a broken wicker chair next to it.

"Set yourself," Papa said as he flopped down at the desk. "Have some Pal."

Drawing orangeade from a soft-drink crate marked "PAL," he snapped the top on a drawer handle and offered Sonny the bottle.

"People drinks it summer an' winter." He laughed.

Sonny took a sip that tasted better than any well water, and a flood of memory came back. He quickly took another, then half the bottle.

"Don't worry," his father said. "Plenty more. Seem like it never run out. Go on—have the whole thing."

When Sonny finished the bottle, Papa handed him another.

"It *is* good," Sonny said.

"Is that."

Papa did not drink, but sat back and seemed to enjoy Sonny's every gulp. As the dust settled out of the light, they sat in good humor, neither saying much of anything, while Sonny burned to know a thousand things. Finally, he got up his courage.

"Papa?"

"Yeah?"

"I tole the game warden you was at Cold Harbor, an' he's saying to me, 'Cain't be.' But I remember—"

Papa laughed again.

"Course, was. Cold Harbor an' more. I was around when whole lotta people die. They jis' pin those notes on themself that they're goin' over an' decide to die, jis' like that."

"For the Grand Army of Northern Virginia?"

"Been with a lotta armies," Papa answered. "Yeah, with the Grand Army of Northern Virginia. Army of the Potomac, too. An' a lot more."

"You was a water boy all that time?" Sonny asked.

"Could say I gave 'em all water."

"How ole was you?"

"I'm about always the same."

Sonny wrinkled his forehead again.

"Let's jis' say we choose to pin that note on ourself, or we don't. We got that choice, but we're gonna find out don't make no difference. None of us goes nowhere 'cuz everywhere's here, you see?"

"Cain't say's I do," Sonny answered. "Why'd I come all the way up here when I could've stayed to home? If'n I stayed to home, I'd be burnt up."

"That's what you pinned on yourself," Papa said.

"Didn't pin nothin' on myself. Jis' got out an' come up."

"An' what you think happen' to you on the way?"

"Well, people got after me, an' I got out the way—"

"An' you saw all them dead animals, an' you had men shootin' at you, an' you found a might of peace with the lady an' the young man, an' you come along an' found your way, an'—"

"How you know all that?" Sonny interrupted.

"That's what I'm asayin'. We all knows more than we thinks, an' we all makes more decisions than we thinks, an' we all needs to see what we really kin know an' what we really kin do, an' then we kin take off all them notes from ourself."

"An' the Tutwilers?" Sonny asked.

"Don't concern yourself about that."

Puzzled, Sonny handed an empty bottle back. In reaching out, he realized the pain had gone from his side. He touched his face, but could not feel the once-tender bruises.

He gestured toward the case of Pal. "Be all right if—" he asked.

"Sure," Papa said, taking the empty in one hand and lifting out a full Pal with the other. As the old man bent over to open it, Sonny noticed three caps on the desk and realized how much he had drunk.

The sun rose well past noon, but neither its heat nor the heat of the forge seemed oppressive. Cars whooshed by, detached from the world Sonny found himself in.

"Takin' you away from your customers?" he asked.

"Cain't do that. Nobody goes away from a good business," Papa answered. "They either needs the fixin', or they needs the water, or somethin'."

"I don't think I kin stay real long."

"Don't matter. All the same, here an' there. You decides what you wants to do all the time anyhow. Same's the men at Cold Harbor. The way it is."

"I belongs to home."

"Where you thinks that is?" Papa asked.

"In the swamp."

"Could be safe down to the Great Dismal or down to Coinjock or down to Elizabeth City—or over to Timbuktu or even to Cold Harbor. That's what I jis' tole you."

"All these places?" Sonny asked, pointing to the Geographics.

"Every one, I reckon."

Sonny relaxed more than he had since Maisie took him in. He thought about his shack and Maisie's kitchen and Hans's garage, and now this drab crowded store seemed like home. He felt better than he had for a long time and freely stretched his arms over his head.

"I'll be," he whispered.

Overhearing him, his father said, "Not 'I'll be.' I *am*. Y'are. Right now."

They sat without speaking for a while when a dull cry came from the barn.

"I loves a case like that. Jis' set back, an' git yourself some rest," Papa said, rising to his feet. Turning the corner he repeated, "I loves a case like that," and disappeared.

Sonny heard an odd, pained voice. Then a short silence, followed by Papa's low pleasant tone, as joyful as he was when Sonny had met him a couple of hours before. The first voice seemed to agree, then argued, and Sonny slipped off into sleep.

The strike of hammer on anvil woke him in the late afternoon, and Sonny got up to join his father. His thirst had disappeared. His aches were gone. His joints worked freely as if oiled, and his steps were strong and light.

"Papa!" he called as he entered the barn. "What's the matter?'"

"Not a thing."

"I heard some callin'."

"Oh, a man comes in here, all cryin' an' achin' an' complainin', an' I tells 'im there's not one bit a truth in what he's sayin'. After a while, he agrees with me an' goes off."

"Ain't that somethin'!" Sonny said. "You never knows with people."

Papa was shaping more metal, and Sonny felt energy run through his body.

"I's wonderin' if'n I might stay a day or two," he said.

"Don't wants you to stay, boy. A day or so, that's okay 'cuz I loves so much. An' I loves that much, I wants you to know what I'm about—I'm really about bein' down to the swamp, too."

Papa laughed at some private joke as he pounded out a new form. Flakes fell off with each blow, and finally he threw metal into the water keg and watched it boil.

"You gotta git that dead metal off, or it jis' won't come," he said.

As he had when a child, Sonny marveled at how Papa could stand by a pile and pick out a crooked piece and heat and beat and cool it into something useful.

"How'd you know to use that hunk, Papa?"

"In my head. I sees it there while it's right under that pile, the whole thing all done already."

Sonny shook his head in amazement.

"Must've took you forever to know how."

"Jis' about."

For the rest of the late afternoon Sonny imitated his father—stared into the junk, made recommendations, pumped the bellows. Toward evening he became good at making choices, and more often than not Papa accepted his choice. He sensed what Papa had in mind and jumped to pull it out. Whatever message his father sent him, he received.

When evening moved in, the forge pit gleamed, but Papa showed no signs of tiring. Sonny, however, began to drag.

"Needs a rest, huh?" Papa asked.

"Guess," Sonny answered.

"Somethin' to eat?"

"I'd be grateful."

"You'll find cans back to the shed, an' a cot."

He pointed to the forge's back left corner, where an opening showed black against the firelight. Sonny walked over and found a shallow lean-to with what seemed to him all the comforts he could want. On a shelf he spotted a hunting knife and cans of pork and beans and hominy. He opened one of each with the knife and ate the contents uncooked.

Exhausted, he lay down on the cot and fell asleep. Three times during the night the hammer woke him. The third time he got up and went to the opening to watch.

"Gonna rest a while?" he called.

"I'm arestin'." The older man showed no signs of stopping.

"Kin I help?"

"Helpin' me by gittin' your strength back," Papa answered. "We gotta lot more talkin' to do."

Sonny returned to the cot, and, as he slept, his father's words echoed in his mind like the sound of a gently touched bell.

CHAPTER 15

Sunlight squeezed into the lean-to through cracks in the boards, falling in stripes across Sonny's overalls. He woke as a rooster crowed far out behind the forge. Stretching in the fast-coming light, he put his feet on the ground.

"Might's well git on."

Entering the forge, he caught sight of his father through a sliding door, unopened the day before. A new savings and loan bound the sunlit yard, and Papa was crouching down and speaking into a boy's ear.

Straightening, he said loudly, "Hear me?"

The boy looked up, but did not respond.

The smith bent over again and said something else in the ear.

"Hear me now?"

"Why, I do, suh, I do!" the boy yelled, jumping up and down and whistling between his teeth as if at a ballgame. He skipped over to Sonny, shook his hand, and ran out of sight.

Beaming, Papa came out of the sun into the barn and gave Sonny a powerful hug.

"Mornin', Papa," Sonny said.

"Mornin', Son. Sleep well?"

"Jis' right."

"Want breakfast?"

"Could."

"Somethin' in the garden back there'd do you."

"Obliged."

Sonny walked out into the dazzling sunshine and around behind the forge where he discovered a garden filled with overripe vegetables—tomatoes, corn, eggplants, squash, and turnips. He picked three golden beefsteaks and ate around the rotten spots, juice and seeds cascading down his chin. He pulled a turnip, wiped it on his overalls, and cracked into it.

"About the best breakfast ever"

When he returned to the shop, a piece of scrap lay in the forge, and his father pumped the bellows, which sounded like a dying man struggling to breathe. Sonny relieved him, watching Papa turn the metal over in the coal.

"Papa?" he said

"Yep." The blacksmith paused.

"What was that boy about?"

"About nothin'. That's what he's about. Said he couldn't hear nobody—in a funny way he had of talkin'. Tole him that's ridiculous. No way he couldn't. That was nothin'!"

Papa's explanation made little sense to Sonny. He again wrote it off to age. The two took up the work, Sonny pumping down and up, and Papa banging on and off until another shape formed and was cast into the keg.

"That's enough. Let's us go for a nice walk around the horn," he said, drawing out the word "nice." "You an' me, we got some kind of talkin' to do."

"Long time since I been around the horn."

They went out through the front doors and turned right along Route 17. Cars, trucks, and an occasional semi sped past, unlike the days of Sonny's youth when only an occasional horse and wagon rolled by.

They passed the three churches that gave Churchland its name: a brick Baptist, a white-clapboard Methodist, and a form-stone Kingdom Hall, once an A. M. E. church. Papa took no notice of them or the traffic, but moved along toward the north and the intersection with the semicircular dirt road dubbed "the horn." Beyond town, it wound through flat farmland, crossed the railroad tracks twice, and circled back toward the blacksmith shop.

Sonny remembered the horn had once been "King's Highway," but the cedar signs were long gone. It had been part of the toll road along the James River toward Portsmouth and made the wide arc to skirt "Trelawny's Curse," a freshwater swamp of quicksand, tangle, and cypress. As a child, he helped sorghum farmers drain the swamp and cut the trees for profit, making way for the straight new road and leaving the old like a dry oxbow.

As they turned onto the dirt, Papa said, "Clear my mind, walkin' around the horn. Thinks of so many things, jis' like I'm all thought. Thinks about things so long ago, an' they seems like they're so far ahead. Not so sure which is which, an' if'n it make a difference."

They strolled up the road twenty feet when Sonny turned to his father. "Papa, how comes you has all this love? Ain't seen you for a long time, an' you act like I jis' been hangin' around."

"Way I am, I guess. Maybe way you is, too, if'n you think about it. You loves the swamp an' the animals an' your friends—"

"Ain't got no friends."

"Got A. R. down the Pasquotank—"

"—how you know about A. R.?"

"Been around. Anyways, why you thinks havin' a lotta people after you's such a good thing? You got somethin' good in you, an' that jis' come out all over. Everythin's your friend. Don't take no people—you see, it's puttin' out all that love all the time that count. It never stop, an' you jis' thinks it has to, or you jis' think you're gonna run out, or you jis' think it has to come back in agin. None of that's the case."

"I never try puttin' out no love," Sonny said.

"That's jis' it. You don't try to put it out there, Sonny, not you. You jis' do it. Don't even know it. Ain't that the beauty?"

The farther they walked away from Route 17, the weedier and dustier the roadbed became. Ragged children, black and white, played on bare board steps or dug in the dust or swung from pecan trees and live oaks as Sonny and Papa moved out from the shanties into the backcountry and crossed the railroad tracks.

A jumpy brown dog joined them, its fur forced on end by ticks, and Papa stopped to tear them out. His hands covered with blood, he threw the ticks into plantain by the roadside.

"Gotta take care of 'em all."

"Dog need somebody."

"Well, got what it need today. That's what count, huh?" Papa said and called to the dog, "Go on, now, Meribah! Git on outta here!" The dog sniffed at Papa, its nose in the air, and made its way up the road.

The two men ambled along in the late-autumn heat until they reached a low cairn, moved there from the entrance to Trelawny's Curse. Etched on a large stone was the word, "Danger." As they approached, they saw a pair of redwing blackbirds land on top of the cairn, watch them, and dart back into a sumac thicket.

"Ain't no curse no more—beyond that now."

"Papa, I wanted to ask you about Mama."

"Don't think I have 'nough love for both a father an' a mother?"

"Wondered where she was."

"Might say she be with you all the time, but you never know it. You got all that love in you, an' that's as good as a mother."

Sonny smiled at the idea. Almost nothing his father said made sense, but he still felt good about it. As they moved on, he thought about why he had had to flee the fire and come home. A. R.'s curiosity was not it. And the fire was not really it, either. Something else had taken control.

"Guess 'tis," he answered Papa's odd comment after a moment.

"You gotta know this about that—ain't no answers in the past. It don't exist."

Even though the sun loomed high, a breeze wafted out of the wilderness from the Curse, and neither Sonny nor Papa broke a sweat. They wandered along enjoying each other's company, talking to a few children along the way and stopping to feed handfuls of grass to a white goat. It reminded Sonny of Honor. Its mistress appeared from a shed and called over to them.

"'Day, Mista Lawton! Visitor?"

"'Day, Missy Mildred. My son, Sonny."

"Spittin' image, I'd say."

"Same stock."

"I kin see it plain. Y'all have a real good walk."

"Please' to meet you, Missy Mildred!" Sonny said.

"Me, too," she answered.

"Missy," Papa said, touching his forehead with his right hand and giving the goat a pat with his left.

"Bye, Mista Lawton! Sonny! Y'all come back."

They reached the apex of the horn, and Sonny felt more rested than when he had gotten up. The breeze kept him so cool he had not developed a thirst.

"Some kind of nice woman, Missy," Papa said. "Could of kilt an' ate that goat like everybody else do, but she love it so much."

"She seem mighty fine," Sonny said.

As the road bent to the left, Papa pointed to a clearing with a log altar in the middle. "There's where we used to have Camp Meetin's 'fore we moved farther along. We have ourself one grand time." Papa snorted. "I remembers once Missy couldn't come 'cuz she's sick, an' she's afraid of the dark.

"The angels was all agoin' home that night, an' Missy was atrottin' to the outhouse in her nightgown with her eyes closed, arms out front of her. She nigh on scared the angels to death. Thought they'd seen a ghost. You never seen so many angels takin' off that night!" Papa snorted again.

"Why a body parade around in a nightgown?" Sonny asked.

"Missy's afraid of the dark. Don't want to look at it." He performed a little sailing dance along the drainage ditch to show what the angels had looked like, tumbled over the edge, and disappeared. Immediately Sonny heard a familiar rattle and ran over to him.

"Don't move! Don't you move!" Sonny yelled.

"Stop!" Papa answered without panic. "Don't do a thing, not a thing! Don't you do a thing!"

He lay on the roadside edge of the ditch and looked calmly to the other side where a fat rattler sank into its coils ready to spring. Its long tail created an intermittent burr—louder, softer, louder, softer.

"Now," Papa said to the snake, "you got your place. I got mine. I'm not agoin' to your place. You're not acomin' to mine. I kin rest here all day an' night 'cuz I got as much cause to be here as you. I'm alookin' at you, an' you're alookin' at me. We somethin' the same."

They watched each other a while, then Papa slowly turned and looked at Sonny. He continued looking at Sonny when the snake began to rear up. It remained in that position for a moment—then, twisting, slipped back over the other side of the ditch. Without hesitation the smithy pulled himself up and in one motion put his arm around Sonny's shoulders.

"There ain't no close calls, far as I'm concerned," he said jocularly, as they crossed the tracks again.

"You coulda—" Sonny exclaimed.

"—coulda, woulda, shoulda…."

They went along, arms over each other's shoulders, until they came upon a stone bench by a fountain, flowing with water from a pipe sticking out of a mossy block of concrete.

"Best water in Churchland," Papa announced. "Never stop, not even in dry times."

He stuck his head under the pipe, washing and drinking deeply. Sonny followed, shaking afterwards like a retriever and spraying his father. Then they sat down to enjoy the splashing of the water.

"Want to ask you about those wars agin, Papa," Sonny said.

"That's another story, boy. We been talkin' all along here, an' I don't think we needs to talk about no war."

As they continued sauntering around the bend back toward the forge, a black girl, hair in cornrows, burst out from a log cabin and ran into the road. She started in the direction of town, but, looking over her shoulder and seeing Papa, she fell, scrambled to her feet, turned, and ran toward them, shouting.

"Mista Lawton! Mista Lawton! Johnnie's dead! Johnnie's dead!"

"Oh, my goodness! What's this?" Sonny looked from the girl to his father.

Papa said nothing, but knelt down to take her in his arms. She cried pathetically and repeated, "Mista Lawton! Mista Lawton!"

"Quiet, chile. What is it?" Papa asked.

"Daddy come home with a load of sand, an' Johnnie hear him an' seen him an' ran out the house, an' Daddy didn't see him an' start to dump the sand, an' Johnnie got under an' got kilt."

"The truck hit him?"

"No, the sand empty on 'im, an' Daddy he hear somethin' an' stop the truck from dumpin' an' got out. Oh, Mista Lawton, come quick!"

"Johnnie out the sand okay?" Papa asked.

"Daddy pull him out an' took him into Mommy, an' Daddy yell, 'Momma! Momma! Johnnie's dead!' Daddy tole me, 'Run, git help!' So I came out the road, an' here're y'all. Come, Mista Lawton, come!"

"What you think I kin do, chile?" Papa said. "Everything's all done already."

"Jis' come, please come!"

"I'm acomin'" Papa said, but he did not hurry.

He and Sonny strolled along as they had been down the dusty road and across the girl's dirt yard. To the rear stood a beat-up dump truck with the bed half raised. As they neared, Sonny and Papa heard wailing and shouting from the cabin. Entering, they caught sight of the sandy little boy on a trundle bed in the back room.

Seeing them, the mother fell on the smith and screamed, "Mista Lawton! Mista Lawton, do somethin'!"

"Oh, my Lordy!" Sonny exclaimed, stunned to find Johnnie was the boy Papa had talked with that morning outside the shop.

"Help us!" the mother continued.

"What you want me to do? Ain't nothin' to do," Papa said with assurance.

The mother shrieked in grief and collapsed at his feet.

Papa laughed. "He's all right, y'all. Johnnie's jis' fine."

Sonny's mouth drew tight in amazement at what his father had said.

"He ain't fine!" Johnnie's father yelled angrily. "He's dead!"

"He ain't," Papa said as he walked into the bedroom. Standing over the boy, the smithy called to him in a slow, rasping whisper, "Johnnie, this be jis' re—action. Come on, boy, git yourself up!"

If Johnnie had been breathing before, it was so shallow no one could tell. As they watched, his breathing became deeper. Everyone stood wide-eyed, saying nothing, watching Johnnie's chest begin to rise and fall.

Papa said, "Come on, boy."

Johnnie, his eyes still closed, whispered, "I hears you, Mista Lawton. But I don't want to."

"Will you listen to that!" Papa exclaimed, grinning at the family. "You're acomin' anyway. Don't have no choice. You got work to do for your mammy an' your pappy."

The boy's body, which had seemed lifeless, began twisting from side to side. Gradually, he drew up his legs and opened his eyes. The family rushed to his side, patting and shaking him until he began to giggle.

"Enough of that," Papa said. "Ain't gonna pin no tags on Johnnie."

He took Sonny by the elbow and led him out of the cabin.

CHAPTER 16

When they got back to the shop, Sonny put his hand on his father's shoulder. "Papa, what you say about Mama don't help a'tall."

The smithy walked over to a group of barrel chairs by the store entry and turned to Sonny. "Some people try to do by shoutin'. I does by speakin' soft. Works better—lessen, of course, you're awantin' to git a dog out the road with cars acomin'. Tryin' to tell you soft what happen' to me, but you wants the shoutin'."

Papa's face turned gray. Its flesh hung heavy, every muscle weak. He put his arms behind him and slowly lowered himself into one of the chairs. Sonny took another.

"Things happen the big men—the doctors an' teachers an' senators—don't understand—don't even allow for. I knows shoein', an' I knows no shoe gonna jump out the keg lessen I pulls it. But some things happen I don't understand, but they happen, so I knows they's possible. Sometime it take a whole lotta sufferin' to find somethin' the big men don't know, don't say's possible. You go through that sufferin', you're in a different world. Hard to tell anybody about it, but you're in it, an' you stays there, even when people still sees you where you was.

"I loved your mama like nothing. We was some kinda twins, 'ceptin' how she feel about Camp Meetin'. Never seen much in it myself, but went after her when she didn't come home that night. Nobody remember if'n she walk back or not. Nothin' to do but go up the horn. Meet her on the way. See if'n she's there.

"She was. Head all atwist, eyes all wide, alayin' all alone so calm on a pile of oak leaves. I knowed she's dead, couldn't help knowin'. I falls down an' puts her head in my lap an' cries an' cries. Never thought nothin'd do me like that. Cries all night into mornin' when a white boy find me. Never thought once about you. Jis' cries an' cries over your mama.

"Well, nothin' to do but git up an' have the nicest funeral with all the trimmin's. An' I did. Did it right—women with the wings an' Preacher Merriot preachin' like he's God Himself right there under the oak. Never heard such preachin'. That night the house burn down like everythin' was after me.

"Still, the funeral over, an' the house gone, an' she well in the grave, I couldn't rest. Couldn't work, neither. Somethin' jis' acallin' me, you know. Beckonin'. Beckonin'. Got out the bed second day an' knowed it was amovin' in the woods up the horn. So I goes along to Camp Meetin' Oak an' sits on one of them benches for the longest time.

"'Twas then it moved on me, such a shakin' an' sufferin' in my heart that I lays back an' thought death himself was acomin' on me. Then I hear Mama say, 'Papa!' I sits right up, an' there she is jis' like always in that feedbag dress with the yellow marigolds on. So I jumps up to grab her, an' she say, 'Don't touch me!' I say, 'How come?' An' she say, 'Listen. Only gotta short time this way. I ain't agoin' nowhere, though, an' I'm atellin' you that. I'm atellin' you there ain' no past, an' there ain't no future, an' there ain't no one place.'

"I reach out, but there was nothin' there. Nobody. What *was* there was whatever made her tell me them things, an' that kept atalkin' in me for a whole day. I don't mean atalkin' like we're atalkin', but atalkin' inside. After that, I wasn't sorry no more. I didn't even think about you agin even though everybody search day an' night. I knowed you'd be all right 'cause of what's atalkin' in me, an' after a few days I could see you, an' I never worried about you agin."

Tears came to Papa's eyes, and he gripped the arms of the chair until his knucklebones stuck out.

"Seen it," Sonny said.

"Seen what?"

"I was at Camp Meetin' Oak."

"Course, you was."

"I seen who done it."

"You seen?"

"'Twas Preacher Merriot."

Papa showed no shock, his face empty except for his eyes, which gazed steadily at the dead forge. He seemed to look into a deeper darkness. Neither spoke for a long time.

"Hammer of God, Hammer of Satan…," he said at last. Again, neither spoke for a time. "…way it often is."

Sonny had known the full horror and fled. Papa only knew half the story, and Sonny left it that way. Searching to change the subject, he broke the silence. "Want to ask you about them wars, Papa,"

"Which?"

"Don't care much what you done or where you been. You tole me you was at Cold Harbor. I knows that. But—them soldiers that die—didn't they *have* to? If'n they could've got away, why they put them scraps on 'em, sayin' where to send the bodies?"

"We goes by what we knows, Sonny," Papa answered, "not by what seem to be. It's what's in your head that's important most the time, not where y'are or what folks are adoin'. That's what come to me from your mama. I knows love, an' I knows you cain't git away from it. Love ain't away from things. Love *give* life. When life become hard, jis' leave out everythin' else. Leave out everythin' but the pauses. Then you start to make your own home an' your own land more than you thinks—no matter where y'are or what's ahappenin'. When you do that, ain't no curse on you, nothin' to hurt, not even a fire or a bullet.

"We lives on, an' everywhere. We needs to know that. I kin see Mama jis' as clear. She move 'round me an' help me like you don't know. It's what I'm asayin'—there's more than our bones, an' it keep on alivin'—there and here, too. When you sees that, you gits the power. Don't come from you. Come from what you knows."

"Preacher Merriot, he livin' on?" Sonny asked.

"Even Preacher Merriot. Everybody come to know the power sometime or other. Might take a awful long stretch."

Sonny and Papa stared at the forge, black now. Night had fallen, and they put an arm over each other's shoulder and said nothing more.

CHAPTER 17

Sonny got up the next morning before the rooster and, entering the forge, saw Papa in the store. Instead of disturbing him, he went right to the dew-wet vegetable patch for another tomato breakfast, as good as the day before.

Low clouds swept the sky as he wandered to the end of the garden, where a thin stream flowed from a drainage pipe. He found cucumbers, picked one, smoothed off the stickers, and chomped on it, making a juicy snap.

"Jis' as sweet," he said.

Blackberries edged the garden's left side, and, although fall had come, shriveled berries still hung along the canes. He gathered them until he had a handful and returned to the forge along the bramble edge, avoiding the butterfly weed that had seeded itself between the rows.

When he turned the corner, Sonny heard a deep voice and stood by the forge doors listening.

"Sure's I 'm a senator and sure's my name's Porter Hardy and sure's Washington's Washington, no letup a'tall in the Middle East or anywhere else for that matter. Not that I see," the voice proclaimed.

Sonny knew a senator meant somebody important and marveled that one had entered Papa's shop.

"Might agree with you," Papa said. "Washington folks thinks all wrong."

In the past two days Papa's comments had been strange, but simple and positive. Now he had changed. He talked about world affairs, talked doubt and doom.

Sonny heard the bellows stretch.

"We can take any country we want—" the senator said.

"—kin do all kinda things, Mista Porta. Not against helpin' nobody, but somethin' else got to happen."

There was a pause, and Sonny waited for some response when Papa continued, "How long you been astoppin' here, Mista Porta, an' we still atalkin' rushin' around smartly accomplishin' nothin'? War after war. How ole is you now? Must be about the old-est person in the whole Un-i-ted States Senate, an' we been ameetin' every time you goes up the route."

"Ninety-three." Hardy's breath labored with exertion. "Appreciate what you say—"

"An' what we been asayin'?"

Sonny peeked around the doorframe as Papa yanked a piece of scrap from the pile. The smithy grabbed one end with a pair of tongs, walked over to the forge, and stirred the coals with the scrap, leaving it in the fire. Sonny could see the gray-haired white senator pulling the bellows stick down, his creased face flushed. He wore a striped tie, striped shirt with gold at the wrists, and striped pants.

"What have *you* been saying? is the question," Hardy answered.

Papa looked at him with amusement. "Needs to give yourself credit, Mista Porter. You an' me both knows there got to be a change in the mind afor' any place else. You an' me, we agrees. Now Washington got to."

"Tole you to call me 'Porter' fifty-five years ago, George—"

Sonny thought of A. R. Lumpkin.

"—Anyway, they're not too intellectual up there."

"Don't mean intellectual, but that, too. I mean a mind more than brain an' more than a body's personality. A mind to love, an' maybe to truly think sometimes. That's the kinda mind."

Squinting at the smithy's words, Porter Hardy pumped the bellows, and Papa, in overalls and leather apron, flipped the metal. They said nothing as he worked it, the senator watching with fascination while Papa hammered and at last threw a shape into the keg.

"Long time before anybody come up to you, George," the senator said.

"Already there," Papa answered. "Jis' don't know it."

Hardy, blushing and shaking his head, retrieved his coat from a bench and folded it over his arm.

"Got to get up the road, George. Love talkin' to you. You know that. Respect what you say. If I could just see a way to use it!"

He and Papa shook hands.

"Will when you're ready. They will when they's ready. Ain't none of us cain't learn."

"Bless ya, George. Be here Christmas?"

"Of course. Be here forever," Papa answered.

Sonny watched them walk like brothers out to the senator's red Cadillac. The senator squeezed in, and the blacksmith waved him off. "Y'all come back!" Papa called as the car slipped into Route 17 like a shrimp boat leaving a wharf.

When the smithy returned, Sonny called, "Papa!" and crossed the smithing floor. "Come try these berries."

Papa approached him with a grin. "Obliged," he said. "Jis' right." They met in the middle by the anvil, and Sonny dribbled the berries into his hands. "Oo-ee!" Papa sounded, putting them into his mouth one by one.

"Almost good's we git in the Dismal," Sonny said.

"Good things everywhere, I reckon."

"An' bad."

"I'm gonna jis' enjoy this treat—"

"Got more than that," interrupted Missy Mildred, who had slipped in by the front doors. "Brought you bread an' jam an' tomatoes an' beans an' you don't know what-all."

"Why, Missy, why'd you—?" Papa asked.

"For you're a good man, Mista Lawton. Goodness itself in my mind. Saw you pickin' that ole dog, an' heared what you done to Johnnie. Why, you're a regular miracle worker, y'are. Always been, Mista Lawton, long's I remember."

"Nothin' but what anybody'd do."

"Not likely!" she said.

No sooner had she spoken than Johnnie's father appeared with a sack of potatoes over his shoulder. The family clustered behind, Johnnie shoving forward and the dog Meribah pushing in among their ankles.

"Come to thank you," Johnnie said. "Kin hear jis' as plain."

His father slung the sack around in front of Johnnie's legs, and Papa's face broke into a wide grin, exaggerated by the white mustache.

"What's this all about?" Sonny asked.

"Tell you what this about," Missy volunteered. "It's about what we do to thank your daddy for being such a good person ever since any of us remembers. Helps out when we're sick. Fix up stuff for us here in the shop. Bring us food when we needs it. Why, he even help the animals—this dog, you know, my goat, cats city folk drops off here when they don't know what to do with 'em. He fix 'em up. He find 'em a home. You don't know what your daddy do! Now, take this all an' *enjoy*." She thrust the gifts in Sonny's direction, and he cradled them in his arms.

"I'll take these over there for you," Johnnie's father said and walked across to lean the potatoes against the store doorway.

"Well, I am obliged," Papa said, still smiling. "Come here, Johnnie. Lemme give you a hug."

Johnnie was too old to pick up, but too grateful to resist a hug from an old man. He grabbed the smith by the waist while Papa reached down to embrace him around the top of his head. Then Papa shook hands with Johnnie's father and looked along toward Missy and the mother and the other children.

"Loves you all. Thank you, thank you so much," he said and leaned down to pat the dog. "Thinks I loves *you* the most."

Papa turned quickly around to the bellows and, without any further courtesies, said, "Got to git back to work."

The visitors filed out with "Bye, y'all's," and Sonny stared at Missy's food on the bench. He hesitated for an instant, then stepped close to his father. "Papa, got to git on home now."

"You're home," the old man answered. "You're home. You're always home."

"Yeah, but gotta git back to the Dismal. Where I lives."

"If'n you thinks so," Papa said. He looked into Sonny's eyes. "But I wants you to remember you was here—that we done a lotta talkin' an' a lotta doin' in a short time. If'n nothin' else, I wants you to remember somebody once said what mos' folks thinks an' does is bubbles. They's two things stand right like stone, Sonny—"

"Two things?"

"Kindness in the other man's troubles. An' courage when you thinks you got 'em yourself."

"Truth to tell!" Sonny exclaimed as he put his hand on Papa's back and rubbed it.

"An', Sonny, I'll be with you wherever you goes. You jis' think out a little step my direction, I'll be acomin' a whole mile in yours."

Perplexed again, Sonny looked through the side doors for a moment and thought about what had happened the last two days. Maybe there was something more in Papa's talk than an old man's rambling. Whatever it was, he felt safe and cared for.

"Jis' look how that food come here to take on your way."

"'Tain't mine."

"'Tis now. You kin go two, three days on that."

"I 'spec'," Sonny said.

His eyes blurred for a moment as he looked from the side yard to Papa to Missy's food.

"'Spec' I got everything I needs to go. 'Spec' don't need nothin' now."

"Always got everything. Don't that jis' show?" Papa said.

"Don't have you."

"Got me in your mind. If'n I'm in your mind, you got me wherever. Food, too. Been sayin' that." Sonny had a conviction Papa's words might all sometime come plain. "I'll be agoin', Papa. Mighty happy I come."

The smith put the food into a canvas bag. He handed it to Sonny, who had brought nothing with him that he had to take away, and so he had food for his journey home as he had had for his journey there. His eyes were no longer misty, and his father's glistened with delight.

Papa put his arm around his son and, with no apparent regret, led him to the shop doors opening onto Route 17.

"You're gonna see things jis' the way they are," he said.

CHAPTER 18

Sonny crossed the road and made his way toward Portsmouth. At a Food Lion, he glanced back and saw Papa still watching. Sonny waved, and Papa waved back. He continued along a fresh concrete walk by the supermarket's parking lot and looked back once more. He thought he saw Papa watching after him and waved again, but he could not tell if the figure waved back.

As he walked, Sonny saw properties like his father's that had not yet been sold off: an unpainted house, the remnants of a confectionery store, a shuttered nursery. Halfway down one block, he stopped to watch a brown dog hurrying through a field wild with Queen Anne's lace. Flat white flower head after flat white head swayed as the dog zigzagged and tossed something into the air. It was Meribah.

"I'll be!" he said. "Come along here."

He put out his hand, and Meribah high-stepped toward him, shaking its toy right and left. As Sonny leaned down to pat it, the dog dropped its toy and pounced on top with both front paws. Sonny pulled it away with a snap and found he was holding a twenty-dollar bill. He had not seen that much money for years and tucked it carefully into his pocket with the pecans.

"You got no use for this, an' here you brings it to me."

He stroked the dog's head and slowly straightened up. With a toss of his arm, as if scattering seed to the wind, Sonny motioned the dog away.

"Home now, Meribah! Home!"

Meribah loped across the lot while Sonny walked back to the sidewalk, turned, and watched the dog weave behind the buildings and disappear as quickly as he had appeared. He knew it would get home without a hitch.

"I'll be," Sonny said again.

With a clamor of squeaking brakes, a Trailways bus pulled up, and its door swung open. Sonny had not known he was at a stop and stared in at the driver.

"Goin' or not?" the driver called.

"Where?" Sonny asked.

"Where-ever!"

"Goin' to the Great Dismal."

The driver's eye squinted as he gazed down Route 17.

"Don't go there."

The door closed, but the bus did not move. The door opened again.

"Take you to the boulevard goes south. Some miles down."

Sonny thought about it, then stepped off the curb and pulled himself onto the bus by the door railing. He passed by the driver and sat in the sideways seat by the steps.

"Gotta pay," the driver demanded as the door closed and the bus rolled ahead. "'About five dollars'll do ya."

Sonny fiddled with the twenty-dollar bill in his pocket—pulled it out, studied it, and handed it to the driver, who gave him back three five's.

"Thank you," Sonny said.

"What's your name, Mista?" the driver asked.

"Sonny."

"Mercurochrome," the driver said with a short salute.

"Mercurochrome?"

"First thing my mammy saw when I's born. Bottle Mercurochrome on the doctor's shelf. Mammy had sixteen of us an' didn't know no more names, so she name me 'Mercurochrome.'" He chuckled.

Sonny smiled, even though he did not know what Mercurochrome was.

"Used to be no blacks set up here," the driver continued. "They set to the back, past the side door. I remembers my mammy, pregnant with brother Booker, she sets down right afor' the door. We jis' been to Piggly-Wiggly, an' we was carryin' so many bags.

"Driver stops the bus right the middle of the street, an' goes back an' tells her an' me to move or git off. We move right to the back fast we can—nowhere to sit, you see. So we jis' stood, my mammy's stomach stickin' all out."

"Yes," Sonny said.

As the bus traveled down the highway, Sonny watched through the window behind the driver—banks, mini-malls, and parking lots raced by like a rushing river.

"Happen once," he said at last. "Papa an' me an' the family went to Virginia Beach in the preacher's car? Jis' settin' there in the sun, enjoyin' the day. Papa's tellin' me about a hunter was such a good shot, had to put salt on the bullet."

The driver looked at him quizzically. "How's that?" he asked.

"Didn't want the meat to spoil afor' he fetched it!" Sonny answered.

The driver exploded in laughter, banging the steering wheel. "Yes, suh! Yes, suh!"

When the merriment trailed off, Sonny took up, "But the po-lice came along said we hadn't no business on the beach. He didn't care we was with a minister—was a white man's beach, an' to git. So we got back in the car an' come 'long home." He thought about it as the bus bounced along. Then he added, "But it's all right."

"All right now," the driver answered. "'Tweren't then."

The bus pulled over to pick up a family of eight, which passed down the aisle to the rear. Sonny ignored them, thinking about his father's words, "Always home…always got everythin'."

He felt at home with the driver, even felt at home on a bus. He had a pocketful of five's and a bag full of food. He knew Papa meant more than that, but that, too, and this began to grow in him.

"We all know more than we thinks," Papa had told him.

He knew he was not going home, but at the same time he *was* going home. He knew he was home now, but the Great Dismal was home, too—and Miz Maisie's and Hans's and maybe the Tutwilers' even.

"Nothin'!" his father had said in the face of calamity, and Sonny was beginning to believe him. He felt Papa nearby. "If'n I'm in your mind, you got me wherever."

The bus trundled on, stopping occasionally to pick up or discharge passengers, all black. Sonny took no notice until a heavy-set woman carrying five shopping bags climbed laboriously up and landed next to him like a large shovelful of wet cement. Her face bloomed round her neck, indistinguishable from her head, and her ankles puffed around magenta tennis shoes. Her permed and gelled hair glistened like patent leather shoes. She wore a faded pea coat over a blue sateen dress.

"'Day!" she said, warping her fleshy neck around to greet him.

"'Day!" Sonny answered.

"Goin' home," she said.

"Me, too."

"That so?" She said companionably, twisting again to catch his eye.

Sonny thought how to respond.

"The Great Dismal Swamp of North Carolina."

At that, the woman slowly shook her head.

"Cain't do that," she said.

Sonny sat up sideways. "Cain't?"

"'Taint there, Mista."

"Where it go?"

"Cain't go there if'n it's burnt to nothin'."

He wondered how she knew. "My home's where I am, ma'am."

"That's okay, but you cain't go where there's nothin'."

"That's jis' it. There's my home, so there's somethin'."

The woman stared out the windows behind the driver, who steered busily through the traffic.

"Never had no home, Mista, 'til my daddy stop beatin' on me an' threw me out the house. I walk right down the street an' on an' on 'til I meets a fancy rooster says he'd put me to work in a cathouse an' give me everythin' I want. Did, too, 'cuz there's where I met my man."

At the mention of "cathouse," Sonny looked at the floor. On a long trek west of Lake Drummond, he had peered into the windows of a whorehouse, where Suffolk boys would roll up Saturday nights in their beat-up cars and lose their virginity. He had asked the game warden about it, and, although it was on the Virginia side, Lumpkin knew all about it and told Sonny he could visit one down by the still toward Elizabeth City.

"Sorry," Sonny said to her, his face tucked toward his shoulder strap.

"Nothin' be sorry about. No sooner lost my beatin'-on-me daddy, got myself a true daddy. Never went home agin. An' then came the little ones. An' now—see these bags?—for my mammy. I takes care of her. She took care of me best she could, but I made out better myself. Don't mind makin' a home for her now."

Sonny said, "Yes."

The bus rolled on until it whined to a stop by a 7 Eleven. The driver reached for the door handle and swung it open.

"Your stop, Sonny."

Sonny craned his neck around the divider and gazed out at a red-and-green sign.

"Where I go?" he asked.

"Right down that boulevard'll take you to North Carolina. Jis' keep on walkin' and walkin'," Mercurochrome answered.

Sonny pulled himself up by a pole and stepped down the two high steps with effort. He looked back at Mercurochrome, who gave him a short salute, and Sonny saluted back. The door shut, and the bus merged into traffic.

Sonny followed the wide avenue past a commercial district and into a housing development. It had been days since he had seen the redtail.

CHAPTER 19

Sonny strolled for two hours until he came upon a bulldozed field covered with stunted weeds as if the drivers had given up. The boulevard ended across the field at a T with a country road. He took it to the right and walked for another two hours until it made a T with an even smaller road by a locust grove. A bent twelve-by-three-inch sign read, "Naked Cr 0.8."

"Laws!" he said and set out for land he knew he would soon recognize. He followed the road for a half mile when it turned to dirt. He would not go all the way to Miz Maisie's or even to the spring. He would cut off when he came to the tulip poplars and make his way south. He no longer had any fear of the Tutwilers. Anyway, he had some idea of the land's lay and of how to skirt the mansion.

He walked along humming, anxious to get back to the swamp, but feeling assured and peaceful. After another stretch, the humming broke into song,

In the sweet by an' by,
when we meets on that beautiful shore,
in the sweet by an' by—

As he sang, he saw a thin white figure coming toward him, leading what looked like a horse. He hopped into a poplar copse to hide and realized it was the same one he had cut through when he came to Naked Creek on his way north. He crouched among thick moosewood and peeked through its broad, pointed leaves. Amazed, he recognized the figure.

"Miz Maisie!" he yelled, tumbling out onto the road. "Miz Maisie!"

Maisie drew back in surprise, and the hinny she led shied.

"Sonny!" she said breathlessly. "Why, Sonny, what on earth you doin' here?"

"Goin' home to the Great Dismal, Miz Maisie. Goin' home!" he shouted, smiling like a child with rock candy.

"Been to see your father, have you?"

"An' more. Him an' the whole town of Churchland. All the folks."

Maisie's eyes widened, and she started to put her hand over her mouth. "I'm so glad for you, Sonny. How was he?"

"Wonderful, jis' wonderful. Everybody love 'im. He love everybody. I loves him, an' he loves me. Jis' like I hoped. I know why I went now, an' I'm takin' 'im with me everywhere I goes."

"Oh, I am glad!" Maisie answered. "I am so glad."

As she spoke, Sonny glanced behind her.

"Miz Maisie, what you doin' with that hinny? I think I knows it."

"Well you might. Belongs to them damn' Tutwiler boys an' showed up by the spring this mornin' when I's out awalkin'. I left it there, but, come evenin', found it agin. Gonna take it into the woods an' slap its behind on home, if'n it's got sense enough to go." Maisie came closer, dragging the hinny by a rope halter.

"Mighty dumb animals, I reckon." Sonny's face puffed with delight. "Oh, I am happy to see you, Miz Maisie! Will you come visit me in the Dismal?"

"Jis' too ole, Sonny. 'Sides, how'd I ever find you?"

"Go down to Elizabeth City an' have the game warden bring you. That'd do. He'd do it, too."

Maisie pondered a moment. "I might, Sonny. Might at that!" She laughed.

Sonny kicked one foot to the side.

"An', Miz Maisie, I ain't afraid no more. I take that there hinny back to the Tutwilers, an' slap it right into the yard. I do that for you."

"You mustn't do that—mustn't!"

"Kin an' will," he said walking up to Maisie and taking the rope. "It'd really pleasure me."

He led the hinny around her and held tight. Then he reached into his overalls pocket and pulled out the fifteen dollars.

"For you," he said.

"I couldn't do that, Sonny!" she answered in a high-pitch. "It's yours."

"Got no use for it. Jis' throw it away. You kin use it. Please take it—here."

He forced the bills into her hand, and she held them loosely, moving her fingers over them like a spider.

"Come for the night, Sonny?"

"No, indeed, Miz Maisie—I gotta keep agoin'. I cain't let nothin' stop me."

"I understand," she said, and she gently pulled his head to her with both hands and kissed him on the forehead.

"I love you, Sonny."

"Well, then," he began hesitantly, "look forward to seein' you." He gazed down at the road, then up again into her face. "Bye, Miz Maisie. Done me a great kindness, an' I does appreciate it."

"Bye, Sonny," she answered, staring at him as tears welled up. She turned back toward the spring, her dress swinging limply at the hem.

"Not agoin' to look, Sonny."

He watched her slim body as she walked a few yards, raised her right hand to her eyes, and lifted her left straight up for a moment. Then he turned, yanked the hinny through the moosewood under the poplar cover, and went his way.

Sonny's legs ached, and he knew he would have to stop somewhere, no matter what he had said to Maisie, but he could not have stayed with her. He wanted to rest on his own terms. As best he could, he retraced his path in the twilight. He remembered the slave cabin in the spent tobacco field and made his way toward it. Night was falling fast, and he looked forward to seeing the cabin as if it were an old friend. When he glimpsed it across the milkweed, he tugged the halter. "Come on, fella! You gits to rest, too."

Sonny's pace quickened over the bumpy earth until he paused by the cabin entrance. He tied the hinny's rope to a log bordered with chink and pulled away a raft of bittersweet, its red-orange berries showering his shoulders and flushing out a band of swallows. He slipped in without hesitating, bent down, and felt for his stalk bed. It was undisturbed, and he crawled on top. He reached into the canvas bag for Missy Mildred's bread and jam and vegetables, ate, and fell asleep.

Birds announced the dawn, and Sonny thought for a moment he was back in the Great Dismal. Eyes closed, he lay still, listening to them, thinking he heard bits of tunes from his youth. Then the hinny pushed against the cabin, sending chink rattling down the inside wall and plunking onto the earthen floor. Sonny realized where he was, turned on his side, and hoisted himself up on a brace from the half-fallen roof, cascading more chinks into the cabin.

Going to the doorway, he looked out into a morning bright on all horizons except the west, where storm clouds towered into the sky. The hinny had folded its legs and slept against the cabin.

"Sure sign of rain," Sonny said, "when a hinny gits down like that."

He pulled the animal up and set off. They walked south, Sonny sensing the land for paths he had taken before. He came upon the apple trees, the sparse fruit more rotten than before. One drop lay under the Maiden Blush with only a side of solid flesh. He ate it for breakfast, a bite here, a bite there, saving the remainder of Missy Mildred's food for later. He pushed the core into the hinny's mouth and walked on, hunting for the oaks and tupelos he had passed through before.

Within an hour Sonny spotted the rounded oaks. The pyramid forms of tupelos would be beyond. He hurried to them and rested against one, figuring the land for where hemlocks might grow and where dells might accumulate water. The trees marked the way and held the promise of a drink from the cistern. Instinct led him on until he saw the tip of a far-off hemlock and broke into a wobbly run. The hinny followed willingly, smelling water.

Halfway there, Sonny crossed a burned clearing of powdered black earth. Fire had died around the edges, singeing only a few saplings. He feared for the swamp, but fixed his eyes on the giant hemlocks ahead.

When he reached them, the hemlocks loomed like a church, limbs curving to the ground and trunks reaching like pillars. He made his way into their coolness and saw the highest cistern at the top of the ravine. Evergreen branches combed the hinny's back as Sonny made for the lowest cistern and dropped his bag. He thrust the green boards aside, jumped in up to his calves, and drank deep draughts from his hands. Cupping the clear, clean water, he scrubbed his face and dribbled it into his hair.

The hinny leaned in, unable to reach. Sonny scooped a double handful of water, lifting it to his chest, and the hinny stretched its neck and sucked it up. Over and over, until the hinny showed no further interest, and Sonny climbed dripping over the wall.

"That'll do us both," he said and gathered the hinny's rope.

He walked in the opposite direction from the power lines, watching out for quicksand as he went. He passed over circles of ash where dry grasses had been and before long found the gray sand, leading into the flats where he had fallen. He turned into the woods on the other side.

Travel was restful this time, and Sonny felt confident he would find the mansion and send the hinny off without being detected. He made his way out of the hemlocks, winding into pines that thinned into brush, where he tied the hinny to a loblolly and crawled through thick undergrowth. As he inched forward, he parted a last stand of brush and peered out. His body quickened.

"Mighty Father!"

The house was gone, burned to the ground but for the two brick chimneys, yet twenty feet from the foundation, not a blade of grass showed signs of burning. The outbuildings, the kennel, the pump—all remained, unkempt but unburned.

"Lawdie!" Sonny exclaimed, his mouth wide. He got up and boldly strode forward. The dogs began to whine. He strolled past the pump to where the rear housewall had been and stared at the ashes. He looked up a chimney to a second-floor fireplace, open to nothing. He moved along the side opposite where he had originally come. Rounding the front corner, he saw that even the columns had disappeared in the firestorm.

He gazed down the clay drive under the oak canopy to the purple-stone walls. There he saw two charred corpses lying next to each other, one with its arm over the other.

CHAPTER 20

Storm clouds mounted from the west as Sonny went for the hinny. He began pulling it toward the house when an enormous thunderclap pounded against the land, causing the dogs to yelp before cowering into silence behind the chain link. The animal jerked, but Sonny held tight, leading it to a shed by the kennel. He forced open the door and fastened the hinny. He found a shovel against a hand-hewn upright and rope hanging from a nail.

As clouds gathered, he knotted together a rope dray and draped it over the hinny, then led it toward the two corpses. The hinny's nostrils flared when the stench hit, but it followed obediently to a task it had done before.

"Good fella," Sonny said, covering its nose and leading it to the windward side of the bodies. He lay down the shovel, dragged the bodies over the dray, stretched them up, and entwined their arms in the net to hold them.

Seared, bloody, and cracked, the corpses were barely recognizable, but Sonny knew they were Harvey and Hal. As he looked down at them, draped like moths in a spider web, he wondered if they had consoled each other while they had lain there, wondered if they had watched the mansion burn to the ground as they died. He thought about the sparks falling randomly here and there and the misfortune of their landing on the house and finding tinder under a shingle or in a gutter.

"Pull!" he ordered the hinny, jerking hard at the halter.

Pulling was its business, and after an abrupt dig-in with its hooves, the bodies, one arm wagging as if greeting, bounced across the avenue of trees toward their parents' graves. Carrying the shovel, Sonny took the hinny to the end of the purple-rock wall and, since the animal showed no sign of wandering off, let the rope trail.

Surveying the two untended graves, he decided to bury the brothers on top of each other, next to Resolve and old man Tutwiler. He set to work, digging in the hard soil, gradually getting down three feet. Sweat poured off his brow. The oppressive humidity fatigued him and intensified the reek of the bodies, so he wandered back to the pump for a drink from the tin cup, still hanging by its chain. Returning to the work, he sat down on the hole's rim, dangling his feet, and gazed in.

"Awful way to die, Papa," he said, scraping a heel in the grave wall. "Why they pin it on themselves I'll never know."

Sonny wondered what his father was doing at that moment, what he would say, what Papa would have done if he had been there before the Tutwilers died. He felt stronger then and extended his arm out on the ground, pushing himself up, and went to digging again. The day pressed on before he could get another three feet down, and he stopped. That was all he could do. He dragged the bodies from the dray and lowered them into the grave as gently as he could. Covering them proved easier than digging, and Sonny had it done by the end of the afternoon.

He stuck the shovel near the head of the grave, untied a rope length, and bound a short branch near the top to make a cross. Stepping back, he bowed his head and clasped his hands together.

"Father," he said, "be with 'em. Love 'em. Guide 'em like you done guided me. Take their feet to you. There ain't no night. It's all day. Forgive 'em, please forgive 'em. Amen."

The sky had turned black, mixed with dirt-yellow clouds. Lightning flashed, and thunder shook the ground. A louder crack cut the air when something had been hit. A hailstone struck Sonny on the head; others bounced off the hinny. A torrent of hail drove into the soft earth of the grave at his feet, sent up puffs in the ruins, and rattled on the outbuildings' roofs. As he heard a shed window shatter, he tore the dray off the frightened hinny, dragged the animal to the barn, and pushed it in.

Then he ran to the uncovered kennel, where the hail pummeled the dogs, and released them. Terrified, they scattered into the woods. One small tan-

and-white, the kind Sonny heard swamp people called a "fyce," scurried behind. The hailstones piled up against the surviving buildings and danced across the yard like demons.

Wind swept in, breaking limbs and downing trees. Chimney bricks toppled into the ashen house site in a series of hollow belches. The second story of one chimney careened sideways and collapsed onto the ground with a deep boom. The shed folded over like a wallet.

Sonny fled back to the barn, and, as he hauled open its broad door, the hinny's hooves struck from inside and threw it wide. With high-pitched hee-haws, the animal raced out with a speed Sonny thought it incapable of. It galloped wildly down through the house site and along the front drive.

Sonny took a few steps in pursuit just as rain crashed down upon him, and he rushed back to the barn and strained to close the door. Inside, skins had been nailed on the walls to cure, edges inky with dried blood. A tawny puma pelt caught light with its silkiness; the bearskin, a hole into midnight. Sonny reached up to touch a stripe on a bobcat coat, then somberly looked away to hunker down in a stall as rain pounded the roof. Like one cymbal clash after another, it beat in shock waves until Sonny thought the roof might break. And it did. A tin sheet blew off the stall next to his, emptying a river into the barn, which flowed in a torrent to the barn door, pressing heavily against it and forming a lagoon.

Sonny decided to wait it out on a hay bale. Reckoning it was suppertime, he reached into the canvas bag for Missy Mildred's bread and jam. He opened the jar, tore off a piece of bread, and poured the jam over it. "I swear," he said cheerfully, "if'n this ain't elderberry." He ate the bread and felt around for a tomato, then a handful of overripe wax beans. "Jis' like Papa's garden," Sonny said as he chewed the raw vegetables, oblivious of the danger.

The rain cascaded in the next stall, and the structure squeaked and swayed. But he remained content for the better part of an hour when the violent storm subsided as rapidly as it had hit. The roof opening still dripped, but the steady flow to the door ceased, and he managed to keep dry on the stall's straw and manure island.

Sonny's sneakers squeezed out water as he got up. He sloshed through the murky rainwater and pushed open the barn door, releasing the lagoon across the barnyard. The landscape was awash, hailstones bobbing where bricks or the pump had dammed them, and clouds bordered an indigo sky.

"Agoin' agin," he said as if nothing had happened.

He made his way across the barnyard, around the foundation, and along the drive, passing the spot where the brothers had lain under the arching trees. He glanced down. The rain had washed over, and no blood stain remained. He looked toward the graves, the mounds eroded by the storm; the shovel-cross stood high, but askew. "God, bless 'em," he said and turned to cut across the cornfield. Puddles had formed everywhere, but the rain was draining off in rapid flows as he came to the road.

When he arrived at the sassafras tree where the hinny had been tied near the carcasses a few days before, there was no sign they had ever been there. The burnt grasses and undergrowth had been washed clean. He wanted at first to avoid the water hole, remembering the butchered wildlife, yet everything looked so cleansed that he retraced his trail to it.

The pond surface reflected the evening sky like crystal, as if nothing deadly could ever have happened on its shores. It was so smooth and inviting that Sonny took off his clothes and sneakers and waded into the bright reflection. He paddled about, washed himself, and floated until the sky became deep violet. He stepped out, shook himself like a dog, and dressed.

A breeze cooled his wet hair, refreshing him. The evening birds began singing while swallows dove around him. It had been a hard day, and Sonny began looking for a place to sleep. He remembered the pin oaks that would lead him back toward Lake Drummond. Walking for a half hour, recalling how he had come, he caught sight of oak shapes in the twilight. He hastened toward them, planning to rest until morning, but the ground squeezed sodden under foot, and there was no dry place to lie.

A burnished moon shone as night closed, and Sonny continued by its light. He was used to navigating by nature, and he had developed a memory for traversed lands, so he trekked on through the mild night, enjoying the moist meadows and dripping trees. Before long, he recognized the piney woods from his northward journey with its well-drained needle floor. Exhausted, he scouted the grove's high ground to settle on its soft bed and fall asleep to the call of a coyote.

Sonny lay there without shifting until saffron lined the horizon. Waking, he felt a flexing against his back. Snake? Bear? Puma? A nudge pressed against his shoulder, and he heard a snort. Cautiously he bent his head up as the hinny's coarse tongue scoured his temple.

"My friend!" he said quietly so as not to disturb the unknown creature at his back. Sonny smiled. "You come back!" He pulled the halter rope down and kissed the hinny's nose. The animal snuggled its snout below Sonny's chin and licked him again.

The frightening pressure against his back moved with Sonny's body as he stroked the hinny. If it was a large snake, a king, he had little concern—but if it was a rattler or copperhead. He analyzed his plight over and over, the hinny nudging and licking him all the while.

Then Sonny made up his mind. Gathering courage, he abruptly jumped up and away as best he could—and heard a rueful yip. Near his feet lay the tan-and-white fyce, asleep. As he bent down to pat it, the fyce bounded up, furiously wagged its tail, and pawed at Sonny's calf.

"I'll be!" he exclaimed. "Believe I got friends for sure!" He grabbed the fyce, tossing it in the air, and hugged it until it yipped again and set to lapping Sonny's cheek.

"Y'all comin' with me to the Great Dismal?" The fyce settled into Sonny's arms as the hinny stood by, watching. "Let's git there soon's we kin."

Sonny collected the canvas bag, fetched a tomato for the hinny, and, emptying the bag, tore off pieces of bread for himself and his new family.

"Missy Mildred feed us all."

CHAPTER 21

Arriving at the upper creek, Sonny pulled the hinny along and headed east. He had not eaten since the day before when Missy Mildred's stores ran out, but his stomach still felt full. The fyce stuck close.

He remembered his father's voice. "You're home. You're always home." The words pulsed though him and brought a vigor he had not known for years.

"Home to stay," Sonny said.

A scree announced the redtail's return, sailing in a drifting gyre toward the east, surveying the land it had fled only days before.

"Happy to see you, ole friend!" Sonny called into the sky, cupping his hands. To him the hawk presaged the return of wildlife to the swamp and rebirth of green shoots even in the late fall. It screed again.

"Hears you, fella. I'm acomin'."

Yet another scree cut the air softly as the hawk flew farther east.

Char, ashes, and black dirt stretched out in front of Sonny as far as he could see. A strange void hung through the swamp—the land leveled of underbrush and trees and empty of swamp creatures. But in his mind it already teemed with life and beauty.

He stopped to remove what was left of his sneakers and threw them away. The hinny waited patiently, and the fyce made a weak effort at retrieval. The still-warm earth pressed between his toes, and he moved to the cool mud of the creek edge.

"The Great Dismal Swamp," he said.

The land took on a familiarity—a collection of low hammocks across the creek like the sleek curves of a puma's body, the wreck of a cypress to the right, a cattail cove ahead.

Sonny squished along for the better part of the day, the sun high above, the creek widening—when a gunshot stopped him. The hinny shied. The fyce shrank down, its head between its paws.

Sonny's legs shivered as he searched the sky. "Oh, my God!" he yelled. He dropped the rope and ran along the spongy shore. "Not my redtail! Oh, please, God, not my redtail!" he screamed.

Another shot sounded, and after an interval, another, and so on, while Sonny, out of breath, slowed, the hinny trailing on its own and the fyce at his heels.

"Cain't be! Cain't be!" he yelled.

Another shot, and Sonny heard a singsong moan, evolving into a call.

"S-o-n-n-y!"

Then, "S-o-n-n-y!" again.

In the distance, Sonny saw a flickering shape. It rose and fell and glimmered with varying intensity. Above it another dull shot cracked, its volume muffled by the absorbent earth.

"S-o-n-n-y!"

He began running again, and the fyce ranged ahead, baying. Sonny knew the voice. "Yah-h-h!" he answered, waving his arms when he saw A. R. Lumpkin stand up in his aluminum boat, seesawing with the shift of his weight.

"A. R.!" Sonny called him by his nickname for the first time.

"Thank God!" the warden answered, jumping onto the creek bank with boat in tow. "Sonny, you're here! Thank God, I found you!"

He pulled the boat up behind him, threw the line down into the ashes, and ran toward Sonny. They embraced like lovers, the warden throwing Sonny awkwardly from side to side. They held each other at arms' length, then, each studying the other's face, burst into laughter.

"Sonny, I'm jis' so happy to see you. Knowed you'd make it. I jis' didn't know how. Where you been, Sonny?"

"Tole you, A. R. 'Tended to go to my Papa, an' I went."

"All the way to Churchland? All by yourself an' no ride?"

"Walk. Jis' like I come in. Walk the whole way an' walk on back, least most the way. Jis' walk an' walk."

"Cain't believe it!" said the warden.

He looked toward the north and then back at Sonny. The hinny came up and shoved Sonny in the back. "Who's your pal?" Lumpkin asked with a smile.

"Ain't got no name. Could give it one. Maybe 'Shadrach.' Yeah, 'Shadrach,' I reckon." Sonny patted the hinny's neck as he had when they first met.

"Seem to like you."

"'Spec' so," Sonny said.

The fyce smelled the warden's boots and rolled on the toes.

"What's your dog's name?" he asked, bending down to scratch its ears.

"Ain't got one neither." Sonny mused for moment. "Could be…could be 'Meribah'," he said at last.

"Meribah? Funny name for a dog."

"Yeah," Sonny said.

The warden watched him stroke the hinny. "Did you see your father then?"

"Seen 'im an' see 'im. Like we never left anytime."

"How you mean?"

"Where he be, I am. That's it. That's all."

"I declare, you're a caution, Sonny! I mean, over to Moyock an' over to Coinjock an' down to Elizabeth City, why, they'll never believe it, not 'til they come here an' see you themself."

"An', A. R.?"

"Yeah, Sonny?"

"Rode a bus!"

The warden chuckled as he leaned over the gunwale for a box of clothes and food. "Did, did you? Well, I'll be! Here, brought somethin' to help you out."

"Don't really need nothin' now," Sonny answered.

"An' you *got* nothin', Sonny. It's all gone. Land's dead. Winter's on us, an' you cain't stay."

"That's what *you* know, A. R. You don't know what I knows. You don't know what I got. Maybe you don't know who I am."

Bewildered, Lumpkin chuckled again.

"Sonny, all these years I've known you, an' I still don't know you. You're somethin' else, somethin' else. You want this stuff?"

"You're a kind man, A. R. I loves you, an' I thanks you. Happy to have it."

Sonny reached for the box and smiled a broad smile. He felt the hammock fill with a love that enveloped him and the warden and the creek and the whole barren landscape.

"Do somethin' for me, A. R.?"

"Whatever you say."

"Go back over to Moyock an' over to Coinjock an' down to Elizabeth City an' tell 'em I'm all right. An' tell 'em they're all right, too. Will you tell 'em that?"

Lumpkin looked perplexed.

"Sure, Sonny, I'll tell 'em. Sure you won't come along with me?"

"I'm home like never before. I got my Papa right with me, you know."

"Don't like leavin' you all alone."

"That's jis' it. I ain't alone, an' I knows I never been. So go on back now, an' tell 'em I'm okay."

The warden stared into Sonny's eyes for a moment, turned around to the boat, looked again at Sonny, and stepped in.

"What'll you do?" he asked.

"I'll be here whenever you comes back. I'll be here about forever, I 'spec'," Sonny answered. "You'll see me all the time."

The warden pulled the boat's bow into the creek, climbed in, pushed the starter button on the outboard, and drifted into the brown channel, turning the boat southward.

"Oh—an', Sonny? Was your father at Cold Harbor?"

Sonny gleamed.

"Yeah, he was!"

Lumpkin shook his head. Gazing back all the while, he steered downstream. Then he opened the throttle and waved a long arms-length wave until he became a shadow against a flat horizon. Meribah followed a stretch, barked, and returned to settle at Sonny's feet.

Sonny gazed up into the blue of a fresh sky. He felt like a new man in a new world. The redtail, with the trailing edges of its mottled wings and rusty tail translucent in the sun, dove up and down, almost touching Sonny's head, and then flew straight up until it was out of sight.

Sonny was surprised to see laughing gulls talking their way north when it was the season to fly south. Mallards, black ducks, Canada geese, pelicans, and flocks of divers flew in, returning to the Great Dismal, drowning out the gulls' jabber with honks and quacks, and clouding the sky with their mass. Blackbirds, mockingbirds, and warblers squawked and sang in bare branches.

A pair of great blue herons with pinpoint-yellow eyes landed by the creek, peered into the water, and speared alewives from a school making its way out of upstream waters to the ocean. A rabbit swam across, scampered by Sonny's feet, and made a zigzag path toward its home.

Deer emerged from among burned tree trunks toward the north and flowed like streams in Sonny's direction, stopping to drink from the creek. Undisturbed by his presence, dozens bounced forward.

Mice and brown river rats scampered under the debris while chipmunks squeaked and darted. A snake slid forward with little interest in the rodents. Bees buzzed along the water's edge among wasps gathering mud to build nests against the coming winter. A hummingbird moth found one dandelion in bloom and drank its nectar, and the earth crawled with insects.

Sonny surveyed the charred land for greenery, put his arm around Shadrach's neck, and leaned down to scratch Meribah's back. Even though fall had long since arrived—from the mud all the way to the border of the woods—he saw shoots and leaves appearing: eel grass, hammock brush, stringy stems of bushes, vines, resurrection ferns, and brambles. Some trees broke with needles and leaf buds, and trees the fire had somehow missed showed even greener.

CHAPTER 22

Through the years that followed, Sonny found that whatever guidance had brought the hinny, the fyce, the redtail, and him together kept them.

And whether because of the fire or some birth or rebirth within him, the creatures of the hammock by the brackish creek lived together in a kind of sacred kinship. Sonny seldom came upon the evidence of bloodshed across the marshes and piney woods. Even the fyce and the redtail seemed content to feed mostly on fish from the creek, and life sustained itself in a closeness and balance he had never known before.

0-595-30987-9